79/=

AFRICAN WRITERS SERIES   FOUNDING EDITOR Chinua Achebe

AFRICAN WRITERS SERIES

158

The Girl from Abroad

The Girl from Abroad

SAMUEL KAHIGA

HEINEMANN

LONDON · NAIROBI · IBADAN

Heinemann Educational Books Ltd
22 Bedford Square, London WC1B 3HH
P.M.B. 5205, Ibadan · P.O. Box 45314, Nairobi
EDINBURGH MELBOURNE AUCKLAND SINGAPORE
HONG-KONG KUALA LUMPUR NEW DELHI
KINGSTON PORT OF SPAIN

Heinemann Educational Books Inc.
4 Front Street, Exeter, New Hampshire 03833, USA

ISBN 0 435 90158 3

Printed in Great Britain by
Richard Clay (The Chaucer Press) Ltd.,
Bungay, Suffolk

Chapter One

You might say I knew her a long time ago. Since she was a baby, in fact. Once upon a time we lived in the same neighbourhood. But I can't recollect ever spending much time with her. She was too young. When I was fourteen she was only seven – far too tiny to be a play-mate. I was strongly built and active. Nimble and sprightly as a ram.

She was a solitary thing with no one to play with. There were no suitable companions for her in either of our families. Neither of my two sisters was her size; one was plump and thirteen and the other one was only four. Besides that a barbed-wire fence separated our two farms and there was a quiet understanding that children of respectable people were expected to stick to their own compound. Everybody in her family and mine kept their own distance but we were polite and friendly to each other. My father always waved to her father across the distance and sometimes the two would walk up to the barbed-wire fence and talk for a good half hour. They could not be great chums, perhaps because my father was at least a dozen years older than hers and was also a good Christian who never drank or smoked. Her father drank and smoked. As he never bothered with the church her mother quite often got a lift from my parents when they went to worship on Sundays, but it seemed to happen by accident as she would never have solicited this kind of favour from us. We were two proud and rather wealthy families, each inclined towards isolation and independence.

I alone was different. I found my own home far too dull, perhaps because I had no brothers at all. I spent a lot of time wandering around in the rough company of boys from poorer homes. I liked to believe I was as tough as any of them. I liked to contradict (if necessary with fists) the opinion that I must be soft because my father was a Court Interpreter and had a car. I wasn't soft at all. At that time I was crazy about her elder sister, a girl three whole years older than I whose breasts had come out; to impress her I would fly over the fence with a pole when she was watching, then shrug off the suggestion that it was dangerous. I did not know it then, but June would grow up to be just as beautiful as her and even surpass her. While I wooed her elder sister she squatted on the ground in childish preoccupation with insects or sand. The elder sister sat under one of the cypress trees peeling potatoes or winnowing the chaff from grains. She smiled mockingly at me, as if guessing what was in my young evil mind. I would lie innocently chewing a blade of grass and all the time trying to see up her silken thighs.

'When will you grow up, Matthew?' she liked to ask me each time I flew over the fence into their compound.

One day I did not pole-vault into that enchanted place but walked slowly in through the gate, my hands in my pockets. A week earlier an Asian doctor had worked on my foreskin and made me a man. I had not been seen trotting around since, I had been lying in bed nursing the pain and waiting for the wound to heal.

She sat leaning back against her favourite cypress tree, looking painfully beautiful . . . looking like June would one day. My manhood was a raw wound between my thighs, wrapped up in bandages and smelling of iodine. It was completely ineffectual but palpitating with swollen desire. I tried not to look up her thighs but she was being deliberately careless. She was, at seventeen, trying to look as sexy and seductive as she could, knowing how it hurt me physically. This kind of thing was allowed by tradition, tantalising the newly circumcised with seductive talk and smiles just for the fun of seeing them squirm with desire and pain. She seemed to know just how hard I had always tried to get glimpses of her different panties and now she let me have a good look and pay with throes from my wound.

I was hardly healed when I said good-bye to the neighbourhood and went to a boarding school. And she never gave herself to me. My first year in high school was also her last. At the end of it she came out and went into the city to work. She sent me funny letters for a while, each time enclosing five shillings for cigarettes. I suppose she felt like an elder sister to me, not like a sweetheart as I would have preferred. But I enjoyed writing back, addressing her as 'Darling Liz' and telling her of my cat-and-mouse games with the prefects. I said I hadn't stopped being fascinated by fences although I was too old and too dignified now to jump over them. I was making holes through the school hedge and creeping away to town to steal some fun. I was a natural law-breaker but I assured her I deserved those crisp five-shilling notes as the academic side of my life was beyond reproach.

She had her first serious affair with a fellow but she didn't mention it to me, fearing rightly that I would be unforgivably jealous. The fellow wasted no time at all in making her pregnant, and she wrote a final letter to me, a tearful letter full of self-reproach about something she had done. She spoke of the meaningless of life and seemed to be toying with the awful idea of suicide. I wrote a long letter entreating her not to do anything drastic. She never wrote again and I waited in fear for news that she had killed herself or run away, as she had threatened, to a far away place where nobody knew her.

'Where nobody knows me . . .' That's what she had written. And June would grow up too and go to places where nobody knew her. Rome, Paris, London, New York, Washington. Where nobody could talk about what she did with her life. I look back and regret the fact that I left her alone in those formative years – and sealed my fate as part of the outer world her conscience would mistrust and reject.

He was a rotten chap. Small and with a scrappy little beard. He hadn't gone to high school but he had a good job. He who had fertilised my darling Liz.

I learnt what had happened when I came home for holidays. I was a lad of sixteen now, always in long trousers and with a hoarse voice in the process of breaking. Everybody was talking about her, Joshua's daughter. They said someone had broken the leg of Joshua's goat. I didn't understand what they meant by Joshua's goat. Joshua had no goats. And then I knew she was the goat.

She was the goat, the outcast, the thankless bitch who had rewarded her father with shame. They made me feel that a curse lay upon Joshua's house, that it was an evil house. At sixteen I was a coward, afraid of haunted houses. I stayed away from Joshua's house and went for long brooding walks alone. It did occur to me that I should pity her and not just mourn the loss of my own dream, but I knew the danger of being seen with her. It was still not clear who was the dirty culprit. For all the neighbourhood knew it could have been me. Me? I demanded, when some hobbledehoys in the neighbourhood wanted to give me the honour. Not wanting to lose all of the glory, I bragged that she and I had done that sort of thing several times, but I had been smart enough to use rubber. Truth was I had shot seed into toilets but never into Fallopian tubes.

I was only fully cleared in the eyes of the youths in the neighbourhood when the real culprit came. The rotten chap with a scrappy little beard. He came during my August holidays, when she was too heavy to go to work but sat with her mother winnowing maize, a maiden fallen from grace. He was surrounded by elders from his area, grim-faced people who had travelled all the way from Muranga, and who seemed to have dragged him there against his will. There was no air of romance, just a sense of duty. Something was being corrected. A curse was being lifted. She was being changed from a limping goat into a woman.

By the scrappy little man and his people.

After they left we heard they had given Joshua over a thousand shillings as dowry, with more to come. The man had also arranged to meet Joshua in town and buy him a suit for the wedding.

A pious neighbourhood heaved a sigh of relief. She had done no evil, no evil at all. Liz was a good girl, had always been good. She was not the type to shame her mother and father. Her man had stayed away so long because he had not wanted to come empty-handed. As for her condition, could you truly blame the young men

4

of these days? Polygamy having died a natural death after the teaching of Europeans, no one could marry more than one wife unless he wanted two pots of poison in the house. Was there then not a little justification, just a little, mind you, in conducting a small test to ensure she was not barren? This seemed to be the fashion, to break the goat's leg first. The main point in marriage, as everyone knew, was to have children. So there might be a point in making sure that a girl missed a couple of moons before going into the great event. Breaking a goat's leg was something that could prevent a great tragedy – the in-laws coming back to complain that they had spent a lot of money on a worthless article.

The wedding was in December and so I could attend it. Some dates stick out. December fifth. A week before Kenya's Independence. Two great ceremonies for the neighbourhood to look forward to.

I was not to be left out. I polished my pointed shoes and put on my sleek jeans. I put on a hat and a scarf. Always dressed to kill, that was me. My dream-girl was being married to a fellow whose face I did not like, but there were other birds to kill.

With dignity I worked my body through the barbed-wire fence and joined the crowd at their home. Tradition said that she must wait in the house with her pretty little maids until he came for her. She was in there now, surrounded by them and waiting. I heard someone say that the bridegroom and his party were one hour late. Someone else replied that the distance from Muranga to Kangemi was not like that from the nose to the eye. We must be patient. He would come for her.

What if he didn't turn up? I thought. The neighbourhood would give a hoarse laugh and disperse. And she would kill herself from shame. The goat with a broken leg.

Are these people from Muranga coming or not? an impatient woman cried. She was dressed in traditional goatskins, dressed for her part, which was to bargain with the bridegroom's people. For a child does not leave her home just like that. Those people from Muranga would have to pay dearly for being late. Kangemi people were very particular about time and did not like to be kept waiting.

Peter Mboca, who was going to give away the bride, paced around and looked at his watch. He was a grey old man in a smart suit, and he was one of her richer uncles. He paced around, his lips moving. He was rehearsing the speech he would make later. How good Liz was ... how very obedient, how hard-working, how bright in school. I stared at his black face and grey moustache. There was something noble in old age. He was about four times as old as I was, I worked out in awe. As respectable people like him must not see me smoking I went and stood behind the pigsty and lit up.

I was smoking when they came. They announced their coming with the aggressive blare of car-horns. Popoooooo. Pipeeeeee. We were not very impressed. Although we could not see over the hedge and the tall maize we could tell, from the sound, that it was a small procession.

I hurried back to see them enter. A Peugeot, a Toyota, a Volkswagen.

A woman spat into the grass. 'Three filthy cars. Not even decorated.'

'It must have been raining in Muranga,' someone said.

True to custom the Peugeot with the bridegroom stayed outside the gate while the other two cars came in. The bridegroom waits in dignity while his best man gets the bride for him.

The cars stopped their ineffectual blaring and out of the Toyota shot a young man. He wore a three-piece suit and had a red flower sticking out from his breast pocket. Smart but muddy, we thought. The rain must have been terrible at Muranga. This must be the best man. Very young chap. Very smart but muddy. We could see he had done his best to wipe the mud off his new shoes.

Another fellow came out of the Volkswagen, leaving others inside. A murmur of astonishment passed through the crowd. This chap was so muddy he should have stayed in the car. He was short and stocky and looked crude.

Our women closed in and asked sarcastically what these muddy people wanted. The shy best man, trying to look as cocky and as brave as a best man should, said they had come for the bride.

Two muddy brave warriors, come for the bride. So!

6

'Is there no water where you come from?' our women shot back. 'Is our girl going to a place where there is no water?'

The short, crude fellow said, 'This is mud, not just soil, mother. It means Muranga is not as dry as people say, but full of water.'

Smart answer. Some women nodded and approved. Muranga was full of water. And water was good.

The slender best man began to explain how 'in fact . . . '

'Don't speak English to us. We are not Europeans.'

He coughed and smiled disarmingly. He was quite a charming young fellow but this was obviously the first time he had got mixed up in these things. He took shelter behind an irresistible smile and started again. Without resorting to English words like 'in fact' and 'actually' he explained that they had got stuck in the mud and had had to pay a tractor to haul the cars out of the mess.

'All right, since you have gone to so much trouble coming here we might give you the bride . . . '

But there were strings. Little things to be paid for. She had broken her mother's pot once and it must be paid for before she was allowed to go.

To our astonishment the two muddy gentlemen sheepishly said they had no money. They had spent their last cent on the tractor, whose driver had taken advantage of the situation to demand a lot of money. Every cent they had.

'We did not come empty-handed, we beg you to understand. But what we had was used up in our battle against the Muranga mud.'

What could one do with such people?

'We set out in much bigger force to come for the bride. But luck has not been with us. Two cars were defeated and are still stuck on the road. Please excuse us.'

The women were annoyed, but Peter Mboca pushed his way forward to calm them. He reminded them that the sun was not still but was moving. And the preacher was waiting.

Rekei tuhikahike, he said. Let us hurry.

We let them have her. The women unlocked the door of her father's house and Liz came out. She was already his, he had bought her. But the marriage had to be sealed in church. Her head was bowed

7

low and I wondered if she was only acting her part according to tradition . . . the sad new bride mourning the passing of the old life. I wondered if at best she felt deeply relieved and happy that it had ended well. I wondered if she loved her man.

We had a few cars standing by and so there was no embarrassment. Joshua and his wife had somewhere to sit. Peter Mboca too. All the bridesmaids had somewhere to sit. But as the rest of us followed on foot to church we could not help feeling that Joshua's pretty daughter deserved a more glamorous show.

This story is not about that particular daughter, and she leaves my pages here. In case you are wondering what happened to her, she lives an ordinary life with her ordinary husband at Eastleigh Section Three. They have four children, I believe, which they can ill afford to keep. Once in a while, it is rumoured he beats her in a drunken rage. You see, although he bought her and even sealed the marriage in church she's got June's streak of independence and rebellion. She outshines him in many ways and he knows it, and does not like it.

As she came out of her house to go to him that day a little girl in bridesmaid's pink followed her, carefully holding the trailing robes of her bridal dress. June Mwihaki, her little sister. I was sixteen and she was nine, delightful that morning but sexless. Now, looking back, I try to remember her face as she held up her sister's robes, just as she had been told to. A small child complying and wanting to please, caught up in a ritual she could not question or fully understand. But she had heard the rumours and the talk of the last few months, and though no one knew it then, it had all made a deep impression on her young mind. Who can tell when exactly she resolved not to follow her sister's footsteps?

As I said, I had known her since she was a baby. When she was born I was seven, and I crept through the fence with my mother's encouragement to go and have a look at the neighbours' new arrival. It was a pretty baby and Joshua's wife allowed me to hold it in my arms.

So it goes that far back, my link with her. I held her in my arms a few weeks after she was born, wondering at the cleverness of God who could make such small wrinkled arms and such minute finger-nails. Her sister was the custodian of the love I would one day transfer to her, this wet, mewling thing whose line of Fate was so complicated.

June. The girl from abroad.

Chapter Two

Let me introduce to you the gentleman I would choose as my best man any time. It's a man-sized job, being a best man, and a beautifully planned wedding can be turned into a fiasco by the inexperience or the inefficiency of a poor specimen. Albert Simon Kago is practical, has a smooth, patient tongue with the old people, drives a hard bargain without offending, and can look as pious as a new clergyman. He would be a great chap to have in the trying affair and, sitting nervously in my car behind some old man's hedge, I would feel easier at the thought that it was the one and only Albert S. Kago handling it.

He's tall and slim and walks with the gait of a man in love with the whole idea of being alive. Once in a while – more and more often these days – you see him in a hat, perhaps to hide that he is going bald at thirty-one, perhaps because a hat enhances the image he has of himself as a 'cool guy'.

I must say he's cool. He has always had nerves of steel. Even as a young boy in Form One he wasn't scared of heavy odds, and he fought back with stones, sticks and fists all those Form Two's who thought they could bully him for being a 'newcomer'.

When we met in high school I was the son of a retired Court Interpreter. His own parents were very poor, and he was being supported through school by an elder brother who was not keen about the task. I suppose I made his life easier. We shared a double-decker, me sleeping up and he down below. He never seemed to have a cent for pocket-money, other than what he needed for shoe-polish, and I had to pay for all the movies we went to. And at night when we sneaked out through the fence it was up to me to order the two beers and to slip a coin into the juke-box. It was the comradeship of those impressionable days that remains the strongest bond between us. Although I thought nothing of those little bills we incurred during our escapades, I was later to realise that he had been deeply indebted and that he was the type who would stay for ever loyal to a friend.

When I went on for A-levels he had to leave school and work in a bank. He was as faithless to his jobs as to his women and was always on the move, looking for something better. Whenever we met he would tell me of the new job and the new woman and how they differed from the last combination, all the time smoking and gulping his drink with fire in his eyes. From his jobs he wanted money, from his women nothing but a good screw. When either became unsatisfactory, as always happened, Albert S. Kago changed as casually as putting on a new shirt. For although he could be loyal it was hard to win him over.

When I went to Canada and America we exchanged a few letters and he told me he had found a good job as an insurance agent. He didn't have to stick in an office and follow a set routine. What he had to do was ridiculously simple for him . . . just convince people to insure themselves. 'Buddy, it's so simple I might be in an orchard picking oranges,' he wrote. 'When I meet a guy who isn't insured I give him a hard time. I have no mercy with anyone who isn't insured. I prove to him that he has no right to eat or sleep or screw his wife. He shouldn't even be around breathing among insured people. He should be among the worms of the underground, the only creatures who might think an uninsured corpse is worth something. Buddy, I can't stand the sight of a two-legged animal going around the streets uninsured. I follow him, pester him, bully him till he has either to be insured or go crazy. I'm not an insurance agent, I'm the Great High Priest of Insurance, and I'm making good money.'

We lost contact while I was working for my MA. For one thing we were too busy, both of us, following different trails of life in different continents. He was still insuring people (I suspected by

11

force) and building up an impressive material kingdom of flats, petrol stations, plots of land and anything else he could lay his hands on. In one of his letters he warned me that I must hurry back from America or stay there for ever. 'This is like a new scramble for Africa. This is a gold rush, buddy. Stay too long over there and when you come back there'll be nothing left.'

Was he the influence behind my decision not to stay on in America and do a PhD? He quoted cases of people I had been at school with and the sort of power they were now wielding, and I must have been impressed – and a little scared for my own future. Anyhow I came back and was relieved to get a job I liked without too much trouble. Relieved to get back to a warm climate and to the kind of lively, almost reckless companionship I had missed abroad.

'Buddy, I'm glad you're back,' he said the night of our reunion. 'Albert S. Kago is at your service. Say where you want to go or what you want to do. The whole town is yours and mine from now right through to dawn.'

I remembered our nights in high school, how we would slip through the fence with an air of excitement and adventure. We were no longer boys but men, but the old spark was still there.

He switched on the stereo tape-recorder in his car.

"I love Jim Reeves, you know. I've got lots of cassettes of his music. When are you going to get your car?"

'The company has promised me one.'

'Good. Nice job they gave you. Assistant Manager. Straight away, just like that. What is it you got? MA Economics?'

'Yeah.'

We drove on, along Uhuru Highway, heading for a night-club.

'Get that car and we have a good time,' he said. 'Did you get a licence while you were in America?'

'Yes.'

'That's good. Here it's tricky, you know. Some guys stand in the way and want you to shell out ten pounds, sometimes more, if you don't want to fail.'

'That's awful.'

'It's all in the game. People have suffered for so long they have told the devil they don't want to be hungry again. And the devil has come up with some fantastic ideas. You know how resourceful he is, the devil. Very imaginative, too.'

'You must have turned to him for inspiration, once in a while.'

'I don't know. These days you never know whether it's the devil you are dealing with or some kind angel. It's a mixed-up world. I just play it according to the rules I find in whatever field I go into. I tried three times for my licence and each time the guy examining me fell asleep with boredom. Fourth time I shelled out what they wanted and the guy woke up from slumber and told me I had passed. It's not my business, I'm not bitter. I suppose the poor bastards have to live.'

We'll draw a curtain over the three years that followed my return from America. They were wasteful. I forgot the frustrations of the western world and fully enjoyed my status as a privileged child of a city that still knew a lot of mirth and warmth. The women and the beer were plentiful and cheap. My salary was in the super-scale. You could enjoy the luxury of driving into the countryside for a live goat that cost only three pounds or so, which you slaughtered and roasted in jovial company outside your quiet mansion at Muthaiga or Westlands. We discovered blocks of flats packed with women who seemed to live in communes and who sold beer in one of the rooms and their bodies in all the other rooms. Sometimes, tired and weary and wanting a change, we moved east into Bahati, Jerusalem and other old African estates to get the feel of the people ... barmaids wiping tables with greasy rags, juke-boxes going off so loudly you had to lean across the table and shout, fights erupting suddenly, forcing you to upset the table and hold it like a shield. Smell of shit drifting in the night air from the sewers, an old man boasting, young clerks arguing, barmaids thanking you for a beer and telling you you were welcome to their houses. The urban people, your own people, separated from you by a vast margin of wealth.

I call them wasteful years, but I don't think we were really blind. Maybe we were seeking for a sense of freedom formerly denied us.

13

We had spent many years of our lives in strict colonial schools where half-illiterate teachers thrashed us like worthless pups. We had spent years in foreign colleges, having to adapt to the discipline of cold, inhibited societies. We were still not really free, but slaves of the companies we worked for – which didn't give us all that money for nothing, which still had their headquarters in London and other places abroad. There was a sense of an unattainable purpose, a sense of constricting frustration. A hopeless lack of a clear direction.

One might as well take advantage of the outlets available. Sex and beer and the ritual of roasting a goat, through which we could feel the illusion of going back to a lost age when men were carefree and got no stomach ulcers.

And not entirely wasteful either, those years. I managed to invest a little money here and there. I kept in touch with my old man and helped him with his business plans. I did not have much time for him but I could feel he needed me. His only son. The man to be entrusted with the territory he had conquered when he was no longer around. The man he would leave behind to take care of the family line and to perpetuate the breed.

I made a move that pleased him immensely. He built a new house for himself and his wife, saying the old stone house he had built in 1955 was too large for him, now that all the children were gone. He asked me if I wanted to move into it and I did so after quite some thought.

I pulled down a wall of the house to include my old bedroom in the sitting-room, which had been designed too small, I felt. I called in some people and they began repainting the walls from pink to a pale blue. I was just beginning to settle down, waiting for a phone to be installed, when it seemed the love of my childhood came back to me.

June Mwihaki, Joshua's younger daughter, returned from America.

Chapter Three

The day she telephoned I was having a little chat with Mumtaz, my Asian secretary. Sometimes after dictating a letter to her I would hang around cracking a few jokes with her. She was cheerful and attractive; her work was neat and efficient. She was mature enough to laugh at my wisecracks without feeling her chastity was threatened. For she could be charming to a man while keeping him safely at bay. When I joined the firm I had found her cheerful inaccessibility quite maddening, but in due course I trained myself to be sexually immune to her; to appreciate her work and develop a blind spot for her beauty and sex.

One small experience we both kept now as a buried secret had helped me develop this immunity. She prided herself on her knowledge of palmistry and one day I challenged her to read my hand. What I gathered from her remarks was that I was rather sentimental, ruled more by the heart than by the mind, quite the wrong type for an Assistant Manager. I would marry rather late in life, due to certain romantic disappointments lying across my path of life, but when I did it would be a permanent union. My life-line was very well developed on my hand and I was likely to have a long span of life. She herself wouldn't live very long because she had a broken life-line.

She wanted to show me the broken life-line but I detained her hand.

'And which line on my hand says you'll invite me to dinner, Mumtaz, and when?'

She laughed shyly and didn't know what to say except, 'Oh, God!'

'I don't even know where you live. It's crazy not to know where your own secretary lives.'

'I don't know where *you* live.'

'I'm up-country now. Seven or eight miles from the city. You wouldn't come even if I invited you, would you?'

'Why should I, Matthew? I'm not your girl-friend.'

'You're supposed to be a thinking, mature, girl, Mumtaz, not a silly baby. You can take care of yourself, can't you? Must a man only have dinner with his girl-friend? Is it not much more worth while to eat with someone of another culture, talking of palmistry and religion and race relations? You know, the kind of things we spend too much office time talking about because you are so un-believably narrow-minded.'

'I'm not narrow-minded. But you don't know about my society and the restrictions imposed upon me. If I was seen with you there'd be hell to pay. I can't do anything I want to do; I can only act as I'm supposed to. If we went out it would have to be in the utmost secrecy.'

Utmost secrecy was the key-word as I crept up to her flat one night. She had at last invited me to dinner. Her parents were away in Britain and she had been put into a flat in a building owned by her uncle. The uncle kept a close watch on her, but tonight he was not around. He and his family had gone to the coast for a short holiday. Mumtaz was sure she was being watched by someone but was willing to risk and afterwards deny.

So we spent a stolen evening in her flat and she gave me some *puri* and *shole*. I'd warned her not to put too much curry into any-thing or I wouldn't be able to eat it. I enjoyed the dinner. A bottle of Cinzano she had bought in her effort to make a drunk's evening complete heightened our sense of intimacy, for she was daring enough to share it with me. Who knows what devil possessed her that night, or what fires of rebellion burnt within her restricted soul? We stumbled into the next room where her bed was, and she only became frightened and hysterical at the last moment. She sprang out of bed and turned on the light of the bedroom. She stood with her head bowed as if terribly ashamed. Then she begged me to go and leave her alone. 'Please don't argue, Matthew. It's no use now. You must go.'

I did up my buttons and left.

But as I went out into the night I wasn't depressed. I had reasons to be happy. First, she had shown she had the same weakness as any other woman, which meant I liked her a little more. Second, I seemed to understand much better the awful consequences I would have left her to face had that weakness led her to lose her virginity. Third, I had been saved from yet another uphill task of deflowering a female, a task that always started off with excitement and ended on a note of depression. For Mumtaz the loss of her purity would have been a catastrophe to regret probably all her life.

It was from that time that we really became friends. We had gone to the threshold of danger and shared the panic. It was almost as if we had had carnal knowledge of each other, of a deeper kind than I had ever experienced before. We knew how two bodies could destroy each other and would in the future keep out of danger.

Our relationship in the office assumed clear boundaries. We enjoyed our jokes, knowing they were just jokes which could go no further. The file marked 'Danger' was permanently closed and put out of the way.

The morning June rang we were joking about her work permit, which was going to expire in a few more months. Couldn't I help her, somehow? She hated having to join her parents in Britain. She had a bit of freedom here that she enjoyed. At least nobody was trying to marry her off to the sons of rich people. Couldn't I talk to my influential friends and have her work permit extended? Didn't I know she was the most superb secretary I could ever hope to get?

'Listen, Mumtaz, I've no influential friends in the Department of Immigration. You either quit the country or become a citizen by marrying me or some other handsome African bachelor.'

'You are a horrible lot, all of you. I'm surprised your wives can stand you when you get married.'

'What makes us so bad, Mumtaz?'

'Mainly drink. Secondly, your incapability to be faithful.'

'Our drinking can be easily explained. We drink mainly because the beer is bloody sweet.'

'Bloody sweet, that stuff?'

'When you get used to it. Then the streets are full of people you know. People you went to school with or grew up with. It's impossible to be lonely the way you can be lonely in other cities. We drink because there is company. And because there's not much else you can do anyway. As for being unfaithful, it's just our nostalgia for the old days when our grandfathers could marry sixty wives if they wanted to. Give us a chance.'

'Give you a chance. . . . There's a girl on the floor below. She's been made pregnant by one of you. A handsome African bachelor And I don't think he'll marry her either.'

'She has only herself to blame. In this day and age no girl in her right mind should get pregnant. Pills are more plentiful than groundnuts.'

'Pills . . . with all their side effects. Must you swallow everything the West invents?'

'Don't Indian women take pills?'

Before she could answer the phone rang.

'Mr Mbathia's office, good morning, can I help you?'

With her hand on the mouthpiece Mumtaz looked up at me and said, 'Another of your pretty victims wants you.'

'What name?'

'I didn't ask her.'

I took the phone. When she said her name was June I didn't know who it was. The name June she had acquired when she was about ten and had learnt the catechism. Offspring of parents who had not 'renewed' their traditional wedding at Christ's altar could not be baptised when they were babies. In the old days I'd known her simply as little Mwihaki. I could not connect the little thing with this feminine voice in my ear.

'So how have you been, Matthew, all these years?'

I tried to hide my bewilderment as I answered, 'Oh, very well. And you?' I hadn't a clue who was at the other end. But the voice sounded very bright, suggestive of a girl full of confidence and warmth.

'Oh, I've been fine. Perhaps you know I went to Washington.'

'Oh, yes of course.'

'Well, now I'm back.'

'Good.'

'I met someone in Washington who told me you were in Stanford. I tried to contact you on the phone but you couldn't be traced.'

Getting more and more interesting. She tried to contact me in Stanford. Who was this girl, for Christ's sake? Why was my memory so bad? Her voice sounded tantalisingly familiar.

'How did you find out I was working here?'

'I was looking for a flat. Someone took me to a friend of yours called Albert Kago. He had some empty flats. He asked me where my home was and I said Kangemi. He asked me if I knew you and I said of course.'

A Kangemi girl. But still I didn't know who she was. You see, it must have been over twelve years since she and I had last spoken.

'When did you come back from the States?' I asked.

'Only last week.'

'I see. I see.' I didn't see anything; I was in the dark. 'And are you working?'

'No, not yet.'

It crossed my mind then that she was a job-hunter who had been told by somebody that I was an Assistant Manager. Maybe she was talking so sweetly to get a job out of me.

'What were you studying?'

'Literature.'

'So you got a BA?'

'That's right.'

Yes, that's right. A redundant BA trying to talk sweetly to get a job.

'Where are you hoping to work?' I asked.

'I'm not so sure I want to work just yet,' she said. 'I had that idea and in fact had an offer from a small publishing firm. I changed my mind. I'm going back to the States to do a little more studying. But before I go back I want to see you about something.'

'You want to see me?'

'Yes. You. When did we see each other last, anyway?'

'Remind me, honey.'

'Years and years ago. I wonder if I'll be able to recognise you.'

Who was she? This conversation was becoming quite fascinating. 'When can we meet?' I asked her.

'When are you free?'

'This lunchtime, if you like. Are you busy?'

'I'm very idle,' she said.

Mumtaz was watching me and smiling to herself. I said, 'We can meet at Brunner's. Sportsman Corner.'

'Yes. I think I know where it used to be,' she said. 'All right. We can meet there. Have you changed much, Matthew?'

'See and be the judge. What about you? How shall I recognise you?'

'I don't think you will be able to. But I'm sure I'll remember you. But if the worst comes to the worst I'm in blue jeans and a bright red sweater.'

'Okay.'

'See you there. What time?'

'Quarter to one.'

'All right. Good-bye, Matthew.'

'Good-bye. See you.'

Mumtaz looked up. 'I fail to see what they see in you.'

'Masculinity, virility, opulence and other virtues.'

'They don't know that you are actually very fraudulent and rather corpulent?' she asked with a grin.

'This one has just come from the States. She remembers me but I don't remember her. We come from the same neighbourhood, but I haven't been in close touch with the people from my place for years. I just can't place her voice.'

I would have rung my friend Albert S. Kago to ask him what she looked like, but he was the type you couldn't get on the phone

20

during working hours. If I wanted him badly I rang his wife at home and told her to tell him to ring me. On a normal day he could be anywhere, attending to one of his businesses or talking a man into buying an insurance policy. I envied him his style of life. That was why he had such a good slim figure. It was a pity to think that at school I was the more athletic of the two, the one in better shape. Lack of exercise and loose living were taking heavy tolls. I could imagine myself at forty and it wasn't something to look forward to. Yet what was the cure? What exercise could I get while confined to the office like a beast in a cage, my only companion being Mumtaz?

Part of the reason I had allowed myself to be persuaded to move up-country was that I felt I might be able to work out my escape from there. I could keep some high-grade cattle or pigs or chickens. You never knew, I might even be able to afford to quit my job and be a full-time farmer. At the moment I had no feeling for the land, but it might slowly come. And then bacon, milk and eggs might replace all these memos, invoices and graphs. Running around selling my own products might help to keep the fat down.

The voice in my ear had sounded nice, and I tried to put a face to it as I drove to Brunner's in the thick, slow traffic that flowed like glue. Yes, she must be pretty. And the fact that she had been abroad was an advantage. *Broad-minded*.

I found somewhere to park with great difficulty and then walked to Brunner's. I entered the Sportsman Corner and almost at once saw her. It was one of the great surprises of my life, for it seemed as if my teenage love, the girl I'd sat with under the cypress trees, had come back to me. Then I looked more closely and realised what had happened.

While I wasn't looking June Mwihaki, Joshua's younger daughter, had been growing up.

Chapter Four

'I must make a confession,' I said. 'When you were talking to me on the phone I hadn't the faintest idea who I was talking to.'

She smiled, the rim of the glass she was drinking from clinking against her teeth. 'Yes, I thought you sounded funny. Rather cold.'

I looked at her fondly. What an achievement! Growing up from a small tot into a woman more attractive than even that sister.

'So you grew up?'

'You thought I wouldn't? You are still funny, Matthew. So I grew up . . . And you . . . So you grew fat?'

I laughed. 'Time performs lots of miracles. You were also in America?'

'Yes.'

'Pity I didn't know. I would have tried to contact you. It would have been very different with you around.'

'I tried to ring you, Matthew, as I told you. Couldn't get through to you.'

'Pity.'

I had always wondered if I had loved that first sister, Liz, wondered if one could love at the age of seven or ten or fifteen. The answer was this excited, rather shaken feeling that had caught up with me now at the ripe old age of twenty-eight. June was doing to me what her sister had so long ago done. Magically tuning the strings of my soul and playing a song. No matter how much I resisted I would have to rise up and dance. For Joshua had brought his daughters into this world to torment me.

A waiter was hovering around us. I stared at the menu and chose something hastily.

'June, what will you have?'

She too made her choice. I gazed at her pretty face as she gazed at the menu. I didn't have to fall in love with June. It had been there all the time, lying dormant.

The waiter left to get our order. I said, 'You look just like your sister.'

'Do I?'

'They used the same formula when they made you two.'

She grinned and shook her head. 'Matthew, you are just as funny as ever. You know you used to make me laugh? And talking of my sister, weren't you very fond of her?'

'Absolutely infatuated.'

'You used to lie at her feet like a puppy waiting for crumbs. You should have known you stood no chance.'

'I'm surprised you remember. You used to be just a kid.'

'Yes, I know how totally you ignored me. But I used to notice things. By the way, why was your father always whipping you? We'd hear the cries from your house and tell each other, "Matthew is being whipped again." Then you would walk casually out of the house, dry the tears and forget. In a short while you'd take your pole and jump over the fence to show us the marks of your father's belt. There was a superb air of nonchalance around you. Hope you haven't lost it.'

'I'm afraid I have.'

'Too bad, Matthew, if you have,' June said.

The food came. I had hardly started eating when she commented, 'I read a Reader's Digest article about overweight people. So watch out.'

'It's not the food, June. It's the lack of exercise. For the last ten years I haven't played enough sport. Don't worry about me, I have a long life in front of me, according to a certain palmist.'

'You believe in that sort of trash?'

'I find it a comforting thought that that palmist might be right. Say, what did you want to see me about?'

'To see how fat you'd become. You see I miss the people I used to know. I've been phoning up people like mad. I want to see them before I go back, for when I do I don't know when I'll be coming back again.'

Sentiments are very strange. That morning I hadn't known June was around. And now I was feeling the pain of having to lose her. I was already scheming on how to get her to stay.

'Why do you have to go back?'

'Mainly to get my MA. But there are other reasons.'

'What if you got a good job? Would you stay?'

'What do you mean by a good job? With good money? You know I'm tired of all this materialism I see around. The only thing that matters to people is grabbing this and grabbing that. I had a circle of friends in the United States. They may not have been ideal but they were already past the stage of futile hankering after money. People could go out and talk. About other things, not just what one is doing and how much money there is in the bargain. I find the crowd here so dull and boring I don't know how long I can bear them. What has happened to people?'

'Don't let it depress you, June. We are just having a rather sharp rat-race of our own. In a few more years things will cool down and people will examine the spoils and perhaps learn to laugh at it all.'

She smiled. 'I'm sure you are not like the rest of them, Matthew.'

'Don't be too sure. One gets carried by the tide.'

'But I can sense you aren't, Matthew. You've got that old air of nonchalance around you still. You can't kill yourself racing after things that don't matter. I can see why you are gaining weight. You've given up all sport. Everything has disillusioned you.'

'I don't know. You could be right. But don't be in too much of a hurry to return to America. There are many here who feel just as lost as you are. And maybe they need company. At least I do.'

She ate silently and thoughtfully.

After the meal we ordered some drinks. She had a second Babycham and I took a vodka. Vodka is good after lunch – it doesn't smell and make your secretary lose faith in you.

24

She sat back, a cigarette in her hand. She had taken a different path of life from Liz who, I supposed, wouldn't dream of smoking and drinking so casually. But how very closely they resembled each other. She was like a twin sister who had decided to linger yet a while longer in the womb. She looked more assured, more confident than her sister had ever looked, as if she had benefited from following after.

She frowned deeply, staring at the smoke from her cigarette. The look on her face and the way she dressed – in the flared jeans and bright red sweater – gave her away as a militant student who had studied all the ways and knew where to go.

She smiled to herself and I wondered what deep thoughts were racing through her mind. 'Yes, Matthew. You have awakened lots of old memories in me.'

'Memories like . . . ?'

'You know – everything. That farm we had. Your father bought it, didn't he?'

'Yes,' I said, knowing it hurt her. From her face I knew it hurt her that the six acres they used to have, with all those cypress trees, now belonged to my father.

'Tell me, Matthew. I . . . this is difficult because it will seem dreadfully naive. I couldn't buy that land back? From you, I mean.'

'Buy the land back?'

'Do I sound sacrilegious? Like a pathetic little fool? You know this was the main reason I wanted to see you. I wanted to ask you to help me.'

'I see . . . Help you.'

'One reason I find it so intolerable to stay here is that it is not the same old place I used to know. To tell you the truth I'm heartbroken. Coming back here and feeling all the life I used to know has been swept away. The house is gone, the farm is gone . . .'

'Your father wanted a bigger farm in Molo. To get it he had to sell his old one to my father.'

'He explained all that to me in a letter. I know the background to it all. I tried to do something from Washington to stop him from selling but he was obsessed with going to Molo. If he had waited I

25

would have raised the money he needed so that he didn't have to sell the land. Do you know what is meant by the phrase "gaining the whole world and losing your own soul"? My soul was there ... on the farm at Kangemi.'

I sighed. She went on:

'My mother didn't want it sold, you know. She tried to stop him. But being a woman she had no power. No power at all. The man is always boss in our society. What my father said had to go. And he was, and still is, a money-hungry, soulless, blundering, vain type of a man. I went to see him at the farm in Molo. He showed me round, swaggering like Lord So-and-so. Showed me all the wheat and the sheep and tried to tell me how much money he was getting. I gave him a piece of my own mind and we parted on not very cordial terms.'

'I see.'

She looked at me suspiciously. 'You keep saying you see. But do you really see?'

'Yes, of course. I see your point of view. Whether I agree with you is a different matter.'

'Where do you disagree with me, Matthew? Tell me. I know I'm a silly little fool and perhaps I don't understand these things.'

While we took our drinks I tried to make her see the other side of things, her father's point of view. He and my father were practical old men who had worked for years and years gathering little pieces of land. During the land consolidation programme of the fifties these little pieces of land were brought together, and each old man saw the fruits of his efforts in one whole.

'You remember the land consolidation and how the little pieces of land your father had all came to your place at Kangemi?'

'Not too clearly.'

'Your land at Kangemi was only a couple of acres. The other four acres were scattered elsewhere. To your father and my father land is not something that came easily, but something that had to be struggled for. They bought their land in small little strips and you can imagine their pride when they saw it all consolidated. You can also imagine their ambition to see it extend. Or to be able to trade it in for something much bigger and undreamt of . . . out there in the west, where once only whites were allowed to farm. To have tried to hold your father back, or to say he was wrong to go is to misunderstand his goal in life. Going to Molo was for him a dream come true. My father also wanted to go. But he has been suffering from high blood pressure and did not want to exert himself with the effort. So he contented himself with buying your father's six acres.'

'Believe me I can see,' she said. 'But aren't we to value anything for its own sake? Must we always keep on moving for the sake of being a little more wealthy? Are we never going to have any permanent roots? Don't roots matter?'

'A man has to keep on searching, hunting for something better all the time. Don't you admire your father for the way he has come up? He will never know poverty again, though he was born in it. There will be enough land for his children when he dies. He has forgotten all about that land at Kangemi. It may be where you were born, but it wasn't where *he* was born. He doesn't feel that same sentimental attachment to it. You must try to understand that.'

She sighed. 'I can understand. But that does not alter the fact that I feel homeless. I was deprived of something I offered to try and buy from him myself, something I wanted to keep. When I was in America I used to dream of our old place and how I would lie on the grass in the hot sun. When I came back I had to sleep in a hotel. Then I found this flat with its silly little garden. Tell me, can I buy our old farm back from you or not? I'm not kidding, I'm serious.'

I shook my head. 'Listen, June. Old men don't sell land just like that these days. My father was very excited when he got those six acres from your father. I doubt if he will ever part with them.'

'Ask him. You bought it for sixty-five thousand shillings, didn't you? I'm willing to go up to as much as eighty, though perhaps not at once.'

'June, he won't sell. I know him.'

Her face fell. She sipped at her Babycham with a forlorn look on her face.

'Look, June, if you have the money there are other pieces of land you could buy.'

'Matthew, it's not just pieces of land I want. I'm not even a farmer. It's my old home I want to buy back.'

'Your old home isn't even there, June. We pulled all the houses down.'

'I could build others. And sentiment aside, I had other, more practical plans. Like building blocks of flats near the road and . . . what are you smiling at, Matthew?'

'You little cunning thing. I knew there was something up your sleeve. The same idea has occurred to me – building flats at Kangemi and sitting back to enjoy the rent without having to report to work every morning. Isn't that what you really want?'

'We are now back to materialism and the whole idea of having to live. But for me it's not just the flats. Sentiment has a place.'

'You'll just have to call yourself a loser, June. My father is a bit too wise to be persuaded to sell. He's quite happy he didn't go west. His land, being near the town, will double in value in a very few years. It's only thirteen acres now but it's very strategically placed.'

June nodded. 'This is why I know I'm not just a sentimental fool. I could see this all along. My father has a large farm there in Molo but although he's proud of it he's constantly worried. He employs people to work and they always run off to better opportunities. The voice that told him to go west may have been not the voice of wisdom but the voice of greed. That's what I wrote my mother from America. That's what my father might realise one day.'

We sat for a while in silence. I felt sorry for her. She seemed to feel so displaced. 'You should try and take it easy, June. Get a job and . . .'

'No. I don't want to get into that kind of routine just yet. Job, flat, pay at the end of the month – that old pattern. I don't want to start rusting away so soon.'

'What do you want to do?'

'Go back to the States now that I have a chance. Work at my books till I can get a PhD. Enter a profession, say lecturing.'

'Ambitious.'

28

'I know I'll make it now,' she said coolly. 'There'll be no nostalgia for home to keep my mind off books.'

When I presented the problem to Mumtaz that afternoon she came out with a simple solution.

'Marry the girl, Matthew.'

'What has marriage got to do with it, my dear Mumtaz?'

'She'll be part of your home. Part of that piece of land she's depressed about. Ah, you Africans and your land.'

I stared at Mumtaz with respect. Her solution could work perfectly, better than she thought. June's desire would be fulfilled, my father's obvious longing for a grandson would be fulfilled, and I would stop feeling like a man between the devil and the blue sea. The devil being my father's fanatical love for land; the blue sea being the Atlantic over which June was threatening to cross in a jet airliner and disappear for ever out of my life. So many birds to hit with one stone. Marriage. And of course the Assistant Manager would have someone sensible and pretty to show off at cocktail parties.

The snag was, did I want to marry June? Did I want to marry anybody?

I had thought of marriage very often and had come to the conclusion it would have to be done sooner or later. Some complication in my mother when the last sister was born had condemned my father to have to be satisfied with one son alone. Just one shaft in his quiver. In my teens I realised that my life could never be mine alone. For example I couldn't just vanish abroad never to be seen again (as I was tempted to do) and I couldn't afford to die in a car accident through fast speeds and too much alcohol. My father being a Christian monogamist would be at a loss what to do. He would mourn not only my loss but also the fact that there would be no one to perpetuate his breed. Yes, the daughters were there, but when daughters marry they become part of other life streams, and they perpetuate someone else's family tree. So Matthew must try and stay alive, until at least he had married and had a son.

Vacating the old house and moving into another had been my parents' way of setting a trap for me. They let me know the house was empty and set me the challenge either of occupying it or finding them a suitable tenant. I introduced several prospective tenants to them before I came out of my ignorance and realised I was insulting them. How could I put in a tenant when they had built another house so that their boy could come home? In other words I, Matthew, had proved by my general conduct in the city that I lacked the maturity and the sense of responsibility needed to build my own house at home and start a family. So with the help of Jesus (who is the cornerstone) the old couple had gathered their resources and built a house for themselves.

And then the challenge is over to you, Matthew. Will you stop wasting yourself in the city and come home or do you want your father and mother to go to an early grave? We have left the old house to you, and you don't need a drop of sweat to settle at home. You wanted to be spoon-fed, you have been spoon-fed. So come home. We have moved to the furthest end of the farm and our fertile maize hides your house from ours. So don't say you will have no privacy. Come home, son.

I went home. But I was still wasting myself in town. Still doing a lot of things my parents didn't like. What fun did I see in the things I was doing? A wife was what I needed, to keep me at home. And there were so many decently brought up girls all around Kangemi. What did I find so difficult?

I sat in the office thinking about it. I mustn't be so selfish with my life. It wasn't my life alone. It had been given to me by my mother and father. I must pass it on. Everyone else did it sooner or later. Even Albert S. Kago, the tough one, had got married and he was saying how lovely it was to hear the voice of a little one calling you 'Daddy'. Even if you were married you could still move around. Look up the old mistresses. There was nothing to lose.

Especially when the girl was as sweet as June.

Yes, marry the poor kid. Save her the trip back to the bleak winters of Washington. Let her have her land. Expand, old boy, be generous with your life. And when you die you will be remembered. For a bachelor dies like a dog.

Get June into your house!

Chapter Five

Two farmers were walking up the hill. My father and I. I had gone down to see him at his new house to see what he would say about June's offer. I knew he would refuse but I had asked June to phone the next morning for a final answer. Although my real motive was to give her a date I had to tell her something.

I was learning slowly to be a farmer. To talk at length about maize and its height, cabbages and their worms, coffee and coffee berry disease, cows and artificial insemination. To talk about rain and when it was due. To talk about weeds and the scarcity of labour. To spot little worms and weevils, enemies of the farmer.

Mbathia senior is about sixty-five. Born in Rift Valley, son of a squatter, and brought himself to respectability through faith in Jesus and hard work. Managed to build a house of stone at a time when most people in the neighbourhood had to be content with wattle and daub and cold shins. Electricity. Piped water. Unheard-of luxuries. Junior took it up from there and went abroad to come home a victorious warrior armed to the teeth with degrees.

A breed to be respected walking up the narrow path through the farm.

'Would you like to see the new coat of paint?' Junior asked.

'Oh, yes, of course. Have the painters finished their work?'

'Yes. Yesterday.'

We walked at a gentle pace to my house. My father, who rarely visited me, was impressed by the progress. New pieces of furniture, the brand new paint. He looked around in appreciation and then sat down.

I had to offer him something. There was plenty of drink around but it was the wrong kind. He never touched alcohol or smoked. These were not the kind of things that had helped the son of a squatter make it in the world. These were the sort of things they were praying every night at their new little house for Matthew to give up. Drinks and cigarettes.

'Would you like some coffee?' I asked. It sounded odd. It always sounded odd, perhaps because of the way he looked at me. It should be my wife, not me asking such questions. I hurried into the kitchen.

I left the coffee pot warming up and went back to him.

'This sitting-room has always looked to me extraordinarily large – since you busted the wall. Is that how you like it?'

'Yes.'

'Perhaps you felt the house had too many rooms you did not need, being alone.'

'No, no. I will no doubt need them in the future.'

I was standing at the window now, looking out. At the cypress trees that marked June's old compound. Poor June. I could understand. When you were in a place like Washington the last thing you wanted to hear was that the house you cherished in your memory had vanished. To erase it from your solitary mind could be painful, especially when you were a woman and sentimental.

I turned to my quiet father. 'Did you know June Mwihaki was back?'

'Joshua's child? Back from America?'

'Yes.'

'Back so soon! She did not stay as long as you?'

'No. But she might soon go back.'

'For more study?'

'Yes.'

'Women are trying hard these days. Some of them even beating the menfolk. Clever girl, June. Where did you meet her?'

'She was shopping in town.' I lied to be on the safe side. 'She inquired about the land we bought from her father. She was eager to buy it back from us.'

My father stared at me in surprise, then laughed.

'Buy it back from us? How amazing! Do they miss it so soon?'

Life was sport. One man competing against another. Joshua had thought he would win by going west but perhaps it would turn out yet to be my father's round. And he was laughing delightedly. 'Don't they like it up there in Molo?'

I wished I had a cigarette. I had them in my coat but I hated offending the old chap. He hated to see anyone burning money. He hated cigarette fumes.

'It's not Joshua. It's June. She says she wants the place back for her own use. She's willing to pay as much as eighty thousand for it.'

He whistled. 'Where do you young people get such money from when you go overseas? We send you to study, you come back with good money. A girl like June we sent away only recently. And she's willing to pay eighty thousand for the land. Tell her it's a good bid but not good enough. The land is worth much more now.'

'How much?'

'Well over a hundred thousand. Joshua did not know what a fortune he was throwing away. He was in too much of a hurry to get into the white men's shoes up there in the west.'

'So are you selling it to her or not?'

He stared at me as if I was crazy. 'Selling it to her? Matthew, how many desperate people have you seen come here looking for a handkerchief of a plot on which to build?'

'Quite a few.'

'Yes, quite a few – and you are rarely at home. If you stuck at home you'd see many more. And my answer is always the same. I'm not selling.'

'Forget it, June. He's not selling,' I said into the phone.

She sighed. 'Too bad.'

'I tried to persuade him,' I said, although I hadn't really.

'Thanks, Matthew. I guess I had better forget everything and just go back.'

Again I felt myself being torn between the devil and the deep blue sea. My father's capitalism, denying a child her little crumbs, and that damned Atlantic. June might never come back to me. Last

33

night lying in my cold bed I had missed her. Driving to work I had thought of her. Hearing her voice had made my heart spring up lightly.

I would marry June. Just for the heck of it. And that rogue Albert S. Kago had better spare some time and be my best man.

'My father came up with one suggestion,' I said.

'Yes, what?' she seized upon the hope eagerly.

Truthfully I reported: 'He said that if you were so eager to have some place to plant you had better give up further education and get a husband.'

Her peals of laughter cheered me. 'Is that really what he said?'

'That's what he said.'

'Tell him if that's the case it might be some time before I plant a single seed.'

'You aren't eager to plant?'

'Not that eager.'

'Oh, June. Not even among the old cypress trees? They are still standing, you know, all thirteen of them.'

Meaning, of course, could she marry me. People work at their own pace and I tend to work rather fast. I get into trouble sometimes for it.

'They are still standing, those cypress trees?'

'Yes. And I think I would like to see you weed and plant among them.'

'Sorry, Matthew. In a couple of weeks or so I'm off from this place. I'm sick and tired.'

'Of what, June? Did I not tell you there are some here who need your company?'

'Maybe I'll be back to them. After a long time.'

She had rejected my offer. But of course we were talking on the phone. You couldn't expect a girl to believe you were serious over the phone. But very soon I would be making a very serious proposal.

For now I got her promise to ring me on Saturday so we could go out, and I hung up the phone. I tried to clear my mind of June and attend to official matters.

34

When I was a small toddler trying to figure out the world and the people in it my father and mother took great pains to convince me that more things existed than you could see with your own eyes. In fact they managed to convert me to their theory that nothing I could see was important. The flowers, the bees, the flies and even the people were not important. There were other things around me everywhere that were much more important. Flying creatures called angels floated delicately in the wind, though I could not see them. Something else called the holy spirit – not to be confused with any other kind of spirit – was just about everywhere. So if I stole or urinated in the wrong place I must realise I was being watched. Watched by creatures and spirits I could not see.

The most frightening of the lot was that fellow Satan. A huge thing like a bat, black as the night and stinking of evil. I must watch out for him. Of course I was never going to see him, but every time I got the temptation to grab a handful of sugar and cram it into my mouth I must know the evil bat was perched on my shoulder. I must shake him with a good thought. I must make him ashamed by returning that handful of sugar or that slice of bread to its place. As I grew up I realised that life was an endless tug of war between your will-power and the hypnotic power of the omnipresent bat. From the number of times I actually crammed handfuls of sugar into my mouth and then ran out wiping my mouth I realised, with genuine concern for my soul, just how weak my will-power was.

The bat, just to trap Matthew, had with his usual touch of genius placed a permanent trap half-way between town and the house at Kangemi. There was a signboard reading 'The Yellow Crystal. Two hundred yards'. Sometimes, while driving home from work in the evenings I remembered the temptation ahead and began summoning all my will-power for the great contest. Rejoice with me when I say that quite a few times I stepped on my accelerator till the speedometer wavered between ninety and a hundred and flew past the haunted place as if that sign had never existed. I thought of the bat, perched on the signboard, his head bowed low in humiliation. The good thought was, of course, 'Tonight I will sleep sober.'

But sometimes I wasn't so lucky. The bat began to hypnotise me when I was still in the office. 'Everything is so dull here,' he would suggest to my mind. 'The only comfort you have is the Yellow Crystal. Five o'clock you'll be there. All your friends will be there. Nice girls will be there. Pass through the Yellow Crystal on your way home. Home? You call that place a home? So silent, so lifeless. You find it difficult to sleep there when sober, don't you? Pass through the Yellow Crystal.'

Having thoroughly prepared my mind, the bat waited for me at the rendezvous and watched me, croaking with glee, as I drove my Ford Cortina through without the least resistance or the faintest nag of conscience. A creature mesmerised.

That afternoon I talked to June on the phone I passed through the Yellow Crystal. I wanted to be alone with a beer, thinking. The uppermost thought in my mind was June and the idea of waking up in the morning to hear my wife June already up and about and humming a tune. Scrambling, poaching or grilling an egg or two for her man Matthew.

Her man Matthew had lost his house-servant immediately he had decided to move from Westlands to the house at Kangemi. I had thought that my presents of socks and jackets and old trousers had for ever won the man's loyalty to me, but I realised how fickle he was when I put him to the test. I asked him to come up-country with me but he shook his head. I told him I wasn't going to the northern frontier but only eight miles up-country, but he didn't want to listen. He stood there with a matchstick picking his teeth and not giving me any reasons.

'I'll raise your pay by a pound if you come up,' I bribed. 'Call it a sort of disturbance allowance.'

He threw away the matchstick and stood there, giving me no reasons. The only thing left to do was to kneel down and beg, kissing the boots I myself had given him – or lose my temper. I lost my temper and we parted. He helped himself to a few socks he felt I didn't need, an old shirt I never wore because the top button was missing; small things like that to remember Matthew by.

This was bachelor life, I thought bitterly now as I sipped a beer at the Yellow Crystal. Bachelor life means having around you troublesome menservants who would cut your throat and not even notify your mother, who would leave you and watch you go up-country alone – uninterested in who was going to wash your shirts, make your breakfast find two matching socks.

I had tried to find another man I could entice to come up-country and it wasn't easy. The healthy up-country air meant nothing to them, the fact that I had electricity left their faces blank, the fact that buses were regular was not of the least interest. They hated going to the country, feeling perhaps that they would rot there and miss other opportunities in the town. They were right to fear: they *would* rot. If I was a manservant myself you would have to kidnap me to take me up-country, I thought as I sipped my cold beer.

Take the silence, for instance. I couldn't bear it myself. Lying on my bed I could hear drops of water falling in the kitchen sink from the faulty pipe. I could hear the footsteps of midnight dogs passing near the window to see if I was hiding some pretty bitches around my house. It was an uncanny sort of silence, especially in the late hours when there were almost no cars passing on the main road. The sort of silence that made you want to reach for the Bible and read again about the Creation of Man. You could understand how Adam felt lying all alone at night, listening to the leaves rustle in Eden, wanting to talk to someone but with nobody to talk to.

I could hear my father's coffee leaves rustling when I leaned over and opened the window to look at stark, complete night in all its glory. A night devoid of encouragement or comment. Night going about its own business like a watchman waiting to be relieved. Like a policeman on the beat, knowing just how many hours he had left. Night.

You tell me to read a book. This I have tried. But it's so silent you begin to suspect that the author is dead and that the whole world is dead and that life was an illusion. You look out of the window but night reserves comment.

'Come on, Matthew,' the bat says. 'Dress up and get out of here. And I'll show you there's still life.'

Sometimes I would yield to temptation and drive off again towards town, to places I knew were open until dawn. I'd grab a woman, tell her to slip that pound into her handbag and urgently come with me. The woman, the bat and I would drive like maniacs towards the house at Kangemi and dive promptly under the sheets. She was bad, she was commercial, she might steal, she was overused but she was still a daughter of Eve. Some were nice and soft, some were very young and even shy, some needed only a little understanding and help. Matthew, being at heart a soft, understanding gentleman gained many friends among them and quite often didn't have to pay them to ease his loneliness. But always he took them away before daylight, so that the neighbourhood did not know.

Psychologists please note that the boy Matthew is not fully to blame. Consider how cruel a mother and father can unwittingly be to their only son. First they teach him to depend on love, then they sentence him to solitary confinement. They expect him to stick around and read, as if he hasn't been reading his ass off for the last twenty years.

Why the hell did they not let him stay in town? If the shoot of a tree has grown one way must it be bent forcibly to grow in another direction? It might snap, might it not, elders? Are we not to move with the times, my people? Are you not the same ones who said that if the tribe did not move with the times it might be destroyed?

What right has anyone to tell the child Matthew where to set his camp? A tree grows and scatters its pollen and its seeds. Is it the concern of the tree, is it the tree's bloody business where the wind should deposit that seed? Then why the hell do you tell young Matthew to come home? Why do you uproot him and bring him back under your shade? Suppose he prefers the free sunshine? Is it your bloody concern?

All right, he's here. Here under your blooming shade. Here in the midst of the dull coffee. Carrying on a monologue with Mr Night. What have you got to offer him?

The room he sleeps in today used to belong to his sisters. Where are they now? Where are those little things who used to fill the house with laughter or tears? Spirited away by the bats and transformed into dull housewives. Where is his mother's voice that used to float, out of key, from the kitchen, singing of the resurrection and such edifying things? It has been replaced by an instrument of torture, that tap dripping in the kitchen. Going tap tap tap.

First you go to a lot of trouble making the boy international. Then you bring him here and begin whittling away at his soul.

All right, he misused his liberty . . . Like that time he lived in sin with the Canadian blonde, and understanding but curiously difficult female. Like the way he used to speed across the bridge of San Francisco in a convertible, regardless of danger to life and limb. . . . Like the Kama Sutra and how he was obsessed with trying out all the postures. Can you prove, in any case, that his curiosity was bat-motivated? Don't give me that shit that a woman must be pinned down beneath the man all the time. Sometimes it's damn good when she is on top of you! And so what if he was friendly with hippies, in the spiritual wilderness of California? Didn't most of the great prophets visit the wilderness to seek for Truth?

Closer home, in Khartoum, while attending a conference for young African managers he took time off to queue at one of the brothels. The Sudanese girls covering their faces with coloured linen to hide them from the eyes of men and the pollution of dust were all untouchable virgins. Should he have presented his paper with a hard on? Our ancestors had many women, remember. A man visiting another across the ridge was not allowed to be bothered by a hard-on. He was given one of the young wives. As there was no such hospitality in Khartoum, what was the boy Matthew supposed to do for two whole weeks? He had to present a paper, remember. And it needed concentration.

Look, we know what you are trying to do to him; we know how honourable your intentions are. He's your only son and you need seed out of him. Good honest seed. You don't want the sort of wild oats he has been planting abroad. You want good honest seed you can see preserved and protected. Perpetuation of the species is your primary concern. It's an animal concern, and therefore honourable.

But Matthew is not a simple animal to be locked up somewhere and encouraged to get his balls busy perpetuating the marvellous breed. Standing on a rather taller hill than you he can see that it's a rather crammed world, anyway, with the threat of nuclear warfare hovering over it like a dark pregnant cloud. The beast Matthew is a clever beast. Grant him that, please. Remember he's got BA and MA and a rather high IQ. Remember he's been abroad and has seen the clouds beneath him like a cosy bed of pure wool. He's a clever beast, a beast that knows danger. Is he to be blamed for hesitating to bring offsprings into a world that might be doomed? Think on it, while you chew the cud.

Chapter Six

Not that I, myself, have never been guilty. Guilty of demanding too much of people. Letting lianas and other creepers grow in the garden of simple relationships. A simple relationship? I've never been involved in one. Plant the seed of a simple relationship, water it with love. Blow the air of poetry on it. But still the lianas of demand and frustration will grow.

I dislike girls who smile at me sweetly and then turn their silly heads away – wanting a simple relationship. I dislike them intensely. They are no use to me.

My father wanted a simple relationship with me. Matthew was to be a small obedient little boy who must read over and over again that bit about the lilies of the field which neither reap nor sow and yet have everything provided for them. It was not supposed to be my concern when I would get a new vest or a new shirt. I was to wait like a nice, patient lily of the field until I was provided for. Of course if the teacher asked for anything special I was to let him know.

He would sit all by himself working out a careful budget in which not a single cent was to be wasted. Being the type that never understood what he was told, I'd begin to whine softly but with increasing vehemence for a new pen I needed. Told to shut up and do my homework, I would begin crying and saying how I wasn't cared for by anybody, how I was required to use the poor lamp for homework and a pen that didn't work properly. My father would try out the pen and tell the jury of females in the house that the pen worked marvellously. That in fact it was a much better pen than the one he was drawing up his budget with. Unconvinced. . . . More certain than ever that nobody in that whole house cared for me, I'd go on snivelling. My father would look up angrily and tell me that he would wallop me like he had walloped me the other night. I would go on snivelling. There was a wound festering in me and I must let the world know. If the world – my father and the prejudiced jury – thought it fit to crucify me they were welcome.

Think of that ripple that came into his conscience a fraction of a second after I had refused to close my eyes for Grace. There they were, all piously thanking the Lord for the food He had provided, while I was still snivelling, a deprived little child. And what did the Bible say? If one of you ever wrongs one of these little ones it were better for a millstone to be tied round his neck.

He was a tough man, but a man of the Bible. Could he be perfectly certain that he was not guilty? That wallop he had referred to. Had the little one deserved it all? What if that millstone was tied round his plump neck some day?

So perhaps it was not surprising that I got most of my demands fulfilled a few moments after they had chorused 'Amen'.

'All right, son,' he would say. 'What is it you said you wanted? Hey, talk to me – and eat your food. Open those mute lips and talk to me, and wipe away those childish tears. You are a man, you know. I can understand your sister's crying but not you. Am I talking to a stump of a tree or to my son?'

My mother: 'Tell your father what you want.'

To her I will talk. It's only a less troublesome type of pen. One that sucks up ink like a syringe and does not need a rubber tube. That's what I want.

What a small pest I was. Totally useless, always demanding. Always upsetting the works. But still to be loved, still to be educated, still to be slaved for.

It could be, I thought, while on my fourth beer there at the Yellow Crystal, we cannot survive in the world if we are afraid of those lianas and creepers that spoil the garden of social harmony.

Wives were demanding but they were still necessary. Children were pests but only for a while. Parents must be treated gently.

I was in love with June. More than I was ever likely to be with any other girl. If fear held me back, if my clamour for the freedom of the soul held me back I would lose the best bet of my life, I might later get married to a much inferior character. A fat barmaid, for example. I could understand June, if I tried. I was sure she could understand me.

Albert S. Kago found me at the counter drinking myself silly.

'Buddy, I knew I might find you here.'

'Oh, Kago, Kago. Have a beer. A beer for Kago. Quick.'

'Yes, buddy. How long have you been drinking? You look as if you are ready to go home.'

'Do I? That's very interesting. I'm only on my . . . my sixth beer. Don't you know my capacity?'

Kago laughed. His beer came and he poured it into a glass. 'I've been drinking too. But not so much.'

I thought for a while. Very deeply, very drunkenly. Then I said, 'Those of you who call me "buddy, buddy", are you really my buddies? Is it lip-service or am I really a buddy?'

Kago said, 'Don't be silly. If you are drunk go home.'

'I want a buddy who can prove he's a buddy.'

'Give him ten beers,' said Kago. 'I'm that kind of buddy.'

'I want the kind of buddy who can take his friend to church and see him properly married. A best man, in short.'

'I volunteer,' said Albert Kago.

'For sadistic reasons, but you are welcome.'

'Who is the girl?'

'June. You know her. June Mwihaki. She's going to be my little walking-stick.'

Albert Kago lit a cigarette. 'Am I to understand that you are engaged after only the day before yesterday, when she asked me for your number?'

'More or less engaged, yes.'

'When did she ring you?'

'Yesterday.'

'And now you are engaged?'

'Let's say I've made an unilateral decision to that effect.'

'Counting eggs before they are hatched, yes?'

'This girl and I were brought up together, Kago. There's a natural affinity between us. She won't say no. Show me a girl these days who will turn down a marriage proposal from an eligible bachelor. It's a favour I'm doing the girl. I'm saving her the trouble of going back to America to bury her head in the sand of books. You saw her, what did you think of her?'

'Okay in looks. In fact I made a pass at her but she wasn't game.'

'She hates capitalists. She's a thinker, you know. With high ideals. Made a pass at her, did you? Shows you what sort of buddies surround me. Anyhow, give me your honest opinion. Isn't she simply smashing? I mean, would you say I was making a mistake?'

Kago sighed. 'When I made up my mind to marry my wife I never asked anybody. I made my own bed alone, knowing I'd never ask anybody to share it with me. Got the message?'

I said: 'Are you trying to tell me that if you found me making a bed you wouldn't help me spread the sheets just because I would sleep on it alone? If I was buying a car and the engine was no good you wouldn't whisper to me? Are you the kind of buddy who would watch me walk into a hole and only come to help me after my leg was broken? There are many who call me "buddy, buddy", but are not really my buddies.'

Albert S. Kago refilled his glass from the bottle and took it to his lips. He swallowed the bitter but indispensable liquid and then set the glass down.

'All right. I can't help you choose a wife, but I can help you buy a car. So, buddy, listen. This car looks just fine. It's a modern car. Sleek and smooth, you know – and fast, damn fast. Do you get me, buddy? The car looks all right. Knowing you like your cars modern, I should say this one looks all right for you. What worries me is the engine.'

'What about the engine?'

'It's one of these liberated engines. It drives off on its own, and the driver's control of it is minimal. When it gets mad it can even decide to eject the driver and leave him by the wayside and go on alone. It's the kind of car that overshadows the driver. The kind of car that feels it doesn't need a driver. A car ahead of its time. The kind of car I personally would try to avoid like the plague. Suit yourself, buddy. It's your money, not mine. Take the car or leave it.'

I emptied the contents of my glass down my throat. Why is our beer so awfully sweet and satisfying? Where shall we end up?

'Kago, listen,' I said. 'This is exactly the type of car I've been looking for. I think I can handle it, I think I'll buy it.'

For those who don't understand the idiom of two drunkards we'll put it in plain words: I can handle June, I'll marry her.

I drove home in the small hours of the night at a speed agreeable to the police, thinking of the cold bed waiting for me and how only June could really transform it into a place worth looking forward to. I felt the sweet feel of surrender. The joy of humbling oneself and submitting to fate. We all had to turn grey-haired, we all had to die. Every human being had a battery of egotism that could be charged and recharged only so many times on the way between Birth and Death. Mine was low that night and I was feeling humble. So what if she was rather wild and militant, a student of Women's Lib? Did that not mean she would always be an interesting individual, someone I could always respect? If a car ejected me and left me bleeding on the road and went on home without my guidance I would have a respect for it. Albert S. Kago wouldn't. He would call the police and have that car towed away somewhere and locked up, then order that it be arrested for trespassing if ever it was seen near his place. People were different.

I must not copy him. I must not imitate. I must not have a passive wife like the one he had. He rolled her over when he needed her. He slapped her when she needed it. She had to wake up, whatever the hour and give us some grub if we came home from some whores, feeling hungry. Like a car she was there to serve him mutely and could easily be changed if the engine knocked. If the engine was operating properly without any funny noises he was very satisfied.

What I was after was partnership. Give me your womanhood

and I'll give you my manhood. Be patient with me. I'm not you, you are not me. Whenever there are two people there will always be two perspectives. If these were the days of polygamy I might not be so reasonable because any time your engine threatened to knock I'd drive that other car. Such luxury we no longer have. You are all I've got and you've got to last me all the way. Till we smash into something and death do us part.

I waited impatiently for Saturday morning, when she was supposed to ring me. Twelve o'clock drew near and she hadn't rung. What a marvellous start! What a fine reward for a man who had surrendered and was giving away his whole life!

'Mumtaz, are you sure a girl called June hasn't rung?'

Mumtaz was sure. 'Sorry, Matthew. But I'm certain you can survive without a girl in your house one weekend.'

'This is my fiancée-to-be. If she doesn't ring I'll go mad.'

'Are you really in love with her or just joking?'

'You are a palmist. Read my hand. My hand is full of little lines that mean love.'

Mumtaz stated at my palm coldly. Then she said, 'I've seen you agitated before, when a girl hadn't rung.'

In pain I said, 'That was the body, Mumtaz. The body with its vices. This is a thing of the soul, and if that bitch doesn't ring . . .'

'You are marrying a bitch?'

Standing tall and dignified I said, 'No, Mumtaz. An angel.'

At that precise moment the phone rang. I grabbed it myself. I just could not stand the suspense of Mumtaz's 'Mr Mbathia's office good-morning can I help you?'

'Mbathia here,' I said.

An unmistakable voice said, 'Hello, Matthew.'

I turned to Mumtaz triumphantly and said, 'Didn't I tell you? She's an angel.'

Chapter Seven

I asked her what she wanted us to do and she said she was in my hands.

'I've got you here in my car and I don't know what to do with you.'

'Drop me at my flat and I'll sleep. Or read an improving book.'

I ignored the suggestion. 'We need to feed you first, don't we?'

'Yes, please. I'm rather hungry.'

'Where would you like to eat?'

'I'm not particular.'

We were driving in jerks and spasms in the thick traffic. I was very happy and contented though someone judging by appearances would have thought Matthew had just made one of his usual quick pickings. She looked cheap and easy-going in her crimplene slacks, loose sandals and a rather crumpled jacket. She was sitting back, her hands in the shallow pockets of the jacket, staring at the riot of midday traffic.

'How can one drive in this chaos?' she asked.

'You just have to. For a while it's a nerve-racking experience and then you get used to it.'

'How about driving out into the country? Some dusty country roads?'

'Romantic. But where do we eat?'

'Anywhere. I don't care, really. I had a sandwich at ten o'clock and I feel all right for now.'

'I have an idea. I don't know if you will like it.'

'I'm sure I'll like your idea, Matthew. You are such a genius.'

She sat there smiling mockingly at me. And at that moment she reminded me again of her elder sister and the way she would smile at me after I had cleared the fence with the pole. One day I didn't quite make it and I hung suspended on the barbed wire and she went into hysterics. Same thing might happen with June. I might try hard to get her and find myself an object of ridicule. She would not be easy to conquer.

'The marvellous idea I have is we go by my place and see what we can dig out of the cupboard. Stale mouldy bread or something.'

'Stale mouldy bread is all right. But I'm not in the mood to meet your folks, Matthew. I have nothing against them, of course, you understand, but I'm not in the mood for small countryside talk.'

'Maybe I haven't explained our arrangement out there. The old house is all mine now. My mother and father built another one right down the other end of the farm. Out of sight and nearly out of memory. There's nothing to worry about.'

'And I was just beginning to admire you for your filial devotion', she said. 'Now I understand what happened. You kicked your old folks out, drove them down the hill. Took over their paradise.'

'No, I plead not guilty. They went down there on their own accord. The children had all gone and the old house had too many memories, I suppose. They built a small cosy one and went down the hill for a second honeymoon. Then they begged me to occupy the big house and not wander around the city. The idea is to subject me to such loneliness in there that I begin thinking about a mate and populating the rooms with children. Pretty ingenious, eh?'

She smiled. 'Sounds quite bright. But you don't look lonely yet.'

'Why should I? I have you in the car with me.'

She laughed and looked away.

We came out into Uhuru Highway and gathered speed. Going up towards Kangemi.

'I haven't been up this way for years', she said. 'I hope you have a handkerchief. In case I feel sentimental and cry.'

We drove on and there wasn't much to say. I thought it wise to leave her with her thoughts. I wondered how deep the wound was in her soul. What would she really have done with those six acres?

She didn't look terribly practical. I cold easily picture her type of paradise. Enough money for food and clothing, and all the time in the world to lie on the grass with an improving book. She had talked of building flats, but only to ensure a constant source of material sustenance. She was a dreamy soul who only wanted to hide from people. She was afraid of the world, the jostling, the bruising of the weak, the arrogance of those who were strong, but she had the kind of strength needed to be alone, away from the herd. A perfect neighbour for me, she would have been.

We came into Kangemi. Lots of cheap constructions along the road. Many of them rented and bringing in good cash incomes to the farmers who had put them up. The city was so overcrowded that anybody with land close to it could make money out of a shack. June had already discovered it herself. And she was right in thinking that if her father Joshua had not been so obsessed with the idea of being a great landowner he could have tapped the gold lying in those six acres. Get a loan, build good flats, place them under company lease. Money would flow in at such a terrific rate that afterwards, if he still wanted, he would be able to buy his precious land in Molo while still retaining his property at Kangemi. I was toying with such ideas myself. If June married me and gave me the necessary push (behind every successful man there's a woman, etc.) we could soon be so rich that neither of us needed to work. And who really cared very much for the pressures of the office?

The road went up a gentle hill and when we were on top of it we saw the tall cypress trees. When we were children carrying satchels they were the sign that we were almost home. To June they stood now as a monument to a life that was no more. I wouldn't have blamed her if she had broken down and sobbed. What is death? It doesn't happen all at once. Before the final oblivion we die and are renewed many times. And some gentle souls cannot bear the full pain of a metamorphosis.

I stopped the car, my agitated signal indicating I wanted to swing right into a drive strewn with whitish gravel, if only that slow truck would pass. A fellow in a VW behind me was impatient, as if he felt that in my situation he would have swung off the road long ago and not wasted anybody's time. The truck passed and we got out of the way and into the drive through my father's coffee. As a bare-footed boy with a satchel I had hated the sharpness of the gravel on a cold morning. Though I had wandered far since then, though I had been so utterly confused and lost sometimes, this place where I had begun my life twenty-eight years before was still reassuringly there. Yes, maybe one could understand June. The elements of her early existence had been blown apart and flung to all the winds, leaving her sensitive soul solitary and bewildered. It would not have mattered much if she had had a roving mind, but I knew from signs in the old days that she was a homely type. A homely type, homeless now.

I parked the car in front of my house.

'Here we are,' I said.

'Mm,' June said smiling, 'I'm not crying, I'm happy. I can see lots of familiar things. It feels good, being surrounded once again by the coffee, the maize, the bananas.'

'Well, out you go.'

We walked round a bit, before going in. We walked to the cypress trees and it was an odd sensation being in the midst of all the maize and remembering the grass and the house and the grunting pigs. But it was in a way comical and we found ourselves laughing.

Laughing at all that silent maize fluttering calmly and unconcerned about what it had encroached upon. Busy pollinating. Over the bedrooms, over the fireplace, over where the foot-worn paths had been. Showering pollen over everything while we stood like fools, out of place. Ridiculously out of place.

We laughed and turned away.

My father being rather a formidable man and strict disciplinarian, we could not quite make our stone house a playground, me and my small mates, but we liked to bounce tennis balls in the verandah when he wasn't there. The concrete floor and the smooth surface of the walls were exciting. We would bounce the balls on the verandah for hours on end, with indefatigable paws and hoofs, until he realised who was responsible for all those dirty marks on the pink walls and gave me a wallop to remember.

June and I ate some fried eggs and bread standing in the kitchen and then we brought out some chairs on to the verandah and sat there sipping some red wine and enjoying the afternoon sun.

'It's perfect . . .' she said, 'so beautiful here. You must feel very proud and happy.'

'It gets lonesome. I miss my flat. I had a very nice flat at Westlands and there were always people dropping in. Nobody ever bothers to visit me here. They have cancelled me off their list and given me up for lost. It's very beautiful here but it makes you very restless. This red wine: I bought it so I could drink it with somebody on an afternoon like this. But nobody ever comes. I have to tell you this. I'm glad you are here. Wish you could come more often.'

She sipped thoughtfully for a while. I noticed the heavy silence that was relieved only by the soft drone of a passing car. A game I used to play when I was ten: turn my back to the road and tell whoever was interested whether it was a Ford Prefect, a Morris Minor, a Volkswagen or a Consul passing. My old man's car was an old Ford Prefect. It was always a matter of luck whether it would start on its own or whether it would have to be pushed. Sometimes it would lie outside the house like a dead beetle, not giving a squeak or an encouraging rattle, till my father went away and came back with a mechanic. But in those days his was one of the few cars around and we were very proud of it.

'You are very quiet, Matthew,' June said.

'It's a quiet place, you know. It's almost as if you have to obey an unwritten rule. "Human beings be quiet, the crops are pollinating."'

She laughed, 'Put on some music, then, if you can't talk.'

I went inside. I put on a Congolese LP. At one time I couldn't stand Congolese music because I couldn't understand the words. But I had gradually got very fond of it.

'How is that?'

'It's a change from the graveyard silence.'

'It's very nice to dance to. Want to try?'

'No.'

'Oh, come on.'

She was reluctant, but I dragged her on to her feet. She got into the mood and we danced to the first three numbers of the LP. Then she sighed wearily. 'Trouble. with them, these Congolese numbers, is that they go on too long on the same monotonous beat.'

'Countryside life is like that. Do you want something else?'

We put on some soul music I had brought from America. We didn't go outside again on to the verandah. We sat on a sofa and listened.

'I feel drowsy,' she said.

'The bedroom is not far.'

She looked at me, biting off a smile. 'I can guess how you spend your Saturday afternoons, Matthew. Pick up a girl in town and invite her for some mouldy bread in your parlour. She comes and gets not just the mouldy bread but also some red wine which you swear has not been touched because you live like a hermit and nobody ever visits you. That touches a soft spot in the girl. When the girl says she feels drowsy from the hot sun and all the red wine you know the charm is working and you tell her casually that the bedroom is not far.'

'Look, as my guest I have to attend to your every need. When you tell me you feel drowsy there's very little I can do other than offer you my humble bed in there.'

'There's a lot you can do, Matthew.'

'For example?'

'Take me for a drive on a dusty country road. Let me sleep in your car while you bump along.'

I sighed. 'Romantic. Any time you're ready.'

I drove June down a dirt road that led towards Ngong Hills. There were large open plains there where nomads once camped with their cattle. Sometimes you see a dilapidated hut standing all by itself before a tiny garden with short, dusty wilted maize. The horizon opens out and you can see for miles. Soon you realise that there are no people around and that you are alone in your car, trailing dust.

Once in a while a small animal flits across the road, delighting you because you have been used to environments too crammed with human beings. So many human beings that if you think of them in terms of maternity deliveries and groaning labour cases you feel flabbergasted.

I could see June getting more and more cheerful. A certain melancholic air around her seemed to be clearing. That red wine had done her some good and she was enjoying the drive. She was no longer sceptically leaning back as if at the heart of everything there was a nullifying hollowness; she was sitting up with her left ankle on her right thigh, her body swaying with the unsteadiness of the ride. She stared straight ahead at the opening road, as if now there was something genuine being promised.

A few more drives like this one, I told myself, and she should get over her depression. She had been back in Africa for over two weeks now. She had spent almost all the time in the congested city, alone and crowded out, feeling she might as well have stayed abroad where one's mind took the lack of space for granted. Here her sub-conscious could not compromise . . . could not accept a certain sense of deprivation that came with having to live on rented premises. Yes, maybe drives like this one, away from the people, would soothe her nerves. Her depression could be traced to people; not anyone in particular, perhaps, but just people with their welter of motives conflicting with her own. Well, more drives like this one. Along dusty country roads of which I knew plenty. Take her to the game park where she can see skipping little bucks that don't think so hard, even if they are constantly being stalked by the cruel cheetahs and the selfish lions that rule the jungle. Every creature is being stalked by something or someone but there is no need to be too depressed.

Somewhere in no-man's-land I drove the car off the road and stopped a few yards into the grass plains.

'We'll rest for a while, then drive back,' I said.

'Yes, certainly.'

We got out. A fresh wind blowing through the plains made her knit up her eyebrows as she tried to shut it out of her eyes.

'How about a walk?' she said. 'I'd like to walk out there.'

'Out there . . . where's out there?'

'Into the empty distance.'

'The world is flat, you know. And over there is the edge of it and we might fall off.'

'Oh, might we? That would be superb. Come on.'

'I'll lock the car first.'

She stood there laughing at me.

'What's so funny?' I asked.

'You've reminded me of a thought I've always had. That when doomsday comes and we are told to get out and line up so that the goats can be separated from the lambs, there'll be a few poor souls who'll take the trouble of locking their houses.'

'And I'll be one of them,' I said with a smile.

'All the goats will lock their houses. The lambs won't.'

I had taken off my jacket during this exchange. I hid it under a seat and I asked if she would like to do the same with her jacket because it was rather hot. She asked me why we had to hide them under the seat and I said it was a precaution. There was a police campaign at the time not to leave anything lying on the seat of a car, tempting robbers. This wasn't the city but you never knew who might come around. I didn't expect anybody from the plains to be smart enough to know how to open a locked car, but they could smash into the glass with a rock. Even in full view of me, knowing they could outsprint me any time.

'Of course they could. You look like you badly need exercises to get rid of that belly.'

'You want to lock your jacket in?'

'No, I don't think so. It's not too hot in this wind.'

I locked the car and we set off. Going towards the wind.

She put her arm through mine. 'Poor Matthew, you are not used to walking, are you? Tell me, don't you play any games at all? Apart from making love to girls, I mean?'

Before I could think of an appropriate answer to that she went on: 'There are so many other things one could do, you know. More beneficial to the mind and body.'

'Like?'

'Tennis, for instance, football . . . I suppose that's beneath your dignity now. You must not be seen running and puffing. But swimming is all right. You can hide your belly under the water.'

'I don't need to hide my belly under any water. And I can't swim, you know.'

'I'm not surprised. I had to learn it in high school. It's one of the disadvantages of not being born near the sea. But when I was growing up I remember I used to see lots of boys swimming in the river. You weren't one of them – those naked slender bodies I used to see? With their little things sticking out. Obscene little boys who called out dirty words to me when I came for water. So you never learnt to swim? Pity. How about golf? There is a dignified game for you. Once I had a boy-friend who was crazy about golf.'

'Golf!' I snorted. 'Is there anything so boring? You hit a small ball, walk after it, hit it again, walk after it . . . It's amazing.'

'How about tennis?' she asked. 'I'm sorry to keep on like this but we have to find a game for you to play. Do you do press-ups and things like that?'

'Once in a while. But I can't bear the boredom.'

'You could turn on the music and press up and down with the beat. It helps.'

'How do you keep in such good form? Dieting?'

'No. I play games. And I do Yoga.'

'Fantastic. Teach me some Yoga.'

'"Teach me some Yoga." Where have I heard that one before? And the guy wasn't the least bit interested in Yoga. He just wanted to see my legs going up. Know what I did to him? I terminated the lessons and bought him a book called Teach Yourself Yoga. He got the message and I never saw him again. Are you really interested, Matthew?'

'Uh-huh.'

'If you have time we'll see what we can do in the few weeks I have. I could start you off, then leave you on your own. I'd like you to learn the *uddiyana*, for example. You learn it in slow stages and at the end of it that belly will have disappeared entirely.'

'Good. Teach me that exercise some time.'

'Yes, it's good for you. I want you to return to being the healthy young lad I used to know.'

A strong gust of wind came crushing against us. June reeled and for a moment stopped in her tracks.

I laughed. 'Being slim is not always an advantage, is it? If it wasn't for me you'd have gone up in that wind.'

'Yes. Maybe I need someone strong like you.'

We walked on through the deserted plains, alone together and happy.

'When do the lessons start?' I asked.

'Right now. Walk tall and straight like a Masai moran. Like the original noble savage. Not like a weary Assistant Manager.'

'Like that?'

'Yeah.'

'Breathe deeply as you walk, throwing your chest out and your belly in. Spinal column erect. Hold your head up and breathe the clean air of the plains. Breath is life, you know. Breathe in deep.'

We walked on and on until we could no longer see the car. Why did we stop? We saw the tree. A tree that, like us, did not seem to belong to the plains – not with its healthy green leaves rustling above the stunted, suffering grass. A tree with a long vertical wound in its shin. A hermit from elsewhere, if trees can be hermits, standing here in the plains meditating and laughing at the absurdity of life.

The tree reminded us we were tired. At its foot was the only shade all around and we were hot from walking.

She lay on her back and looked at the restless leaves that threw a shade upon her face and breast. A tattered shade, the best the hermit of the plains could offer. 'How does it stay so green?' she inquired.

'I can't tell.'

'I suppose its roots are deep,' she said. 'They must be deep, or how else . . .?' She closed her eyes, shutting out the leaves and the sky. Shutting me also out of her inner world, but with the assurance that we were there and would not vanish when she wasn't looking. Supine and at peace.

'Tired?'

For a moment she opened her eyelids for a polite intake of us, and closed them again with a self-exonerating smile.

'It's that red wine. And the heat.'

So we were supposed to wait, while she slept, the patient tree and I. Keep watch while she slept and drive all the wild nomads away. The prerogative of Woman. It's a crowded world now but it would be as empty as these desolate plains if we left initiative to the woman. There she lies with her eyes closed. Pathetic.

Am I spoiling an idyllic African moment with a filthy thought? Judge me like you'd judge the fly on your breakfast table. It springs on its female and makes frantic love before your hand of wrath descends to take two frail lives. Not because of procreation, but because of contamination. The happy flies!

And yet as I watch over her and search in the nooks and crannies of a frustrated conscience I cannot be sure that my eagerness is right and her indifference wrong. I have never been a woman, never felt remotely like one. What I have in my ready pouch is mature seed. Millions or billions of minute little fish that wriggle their tails in the desperation of their imprisonment. Given the slightest chance, given any moist hole, I'll inject them and set myself and them free. Set them free to swim, those clever things that live in oceans within me, to swim with desperate strokes along rivers of life within her. Each fighting for survival, fighting to become human and live. Racing towards the great goal that lies hidden within June. She holds the key and must be responsible. She's the mother of the race and I'm but a fretful child and ever shall be. A fretful child. Woman's child.

Treat sex with caution. Talk about hermits. I knew one when I was eleven or twelve. He lived alone in something like an igloo, a a childish construction of sticks and elephant grass. Too old for sex or disillusioned with it. He used to smelt iron from some mysterious type of earth. Geography teacher said there was no iron ore in Kenya, but this clever son of a gun had all the iron he needed. He was a blacksmith working with bellows. He made spears and swords, and it was rumoured he used to confer with forest fighters in the middle of the night. But he was never suspected by the authorities and was never arrested. Going home from school we would pass through the plains to where he was camped and squat at the doorway, coughing from the fumes. We'd ask him where he got the iron from and he would only chuckle. It used to be a secretive business, the blacksmith's trade, and the knowledge was passed from father to son and protected by an aura of magic. We would poke our young bright educated noses into his igloo and question him slowly. Teacher says there's no iron ore in Kenya, where do you get yours? He would chuckle again. He was under oath never to tell a stranger.

He must be dead, if only of heart-break. How could he survive the influx of shining steel from Manchester and Sheffield? And then it became illegal to carry bows and arrows and swords, under the dangerous weapons act. No blacksmith with self-respect could survive the humiliation.

Yet once he had a special place in the life of a community. He was displaced and cast away into the plains to become a bit of a laughing-stock.

Culture is not stagnant like the water of the marshes that breed germs. Maybe that is what someone should have told the old guy.

She slept for an hour or so while I waited patiently, the kind wind of the plains lapping the sweat of my brow. Then she opened her eyes and looked momentarily startled to see me there.

'Hello,' I said. 'Back with us again?

She smiled ruefully. She rubbed her eyes and then sat up.

'I'm sorry. I didn't mean to sleep. Am I not horrible?'

'Sleep is all right. All girls need their beauty sleep anyway.'

'Sleeping on our first time out together.' She slapped me on the back affectionately. 'I suppose it only goes to show how very dull you are.'

'Yes, I know.'

'Oh, Matthew. I didn't mean that. You are sweet. The reason I slept is that I have been losing sleep lately thinking of a lot of things. Does that make you feel better?'

'You didn't upset me by sleeping. If you want to sleep some more feel free.'

58

Her eyes searched my face, trying to see if I was mocking her.

'You have become very tame and gentle,' she said. 'You didn't grow up into what someone would have expected. Where has the dare-devil gone to?'

'The world took him by the tail and dashed his brains against a concrete wall.'

'And now you are very very tame?'

'Yes.'

'Yet when I look into your eyes I find them strange. Where did I read this – that the eyes are the windows of the soul? Must be some book on Primitive Culture. In some primitive art-form the eyes were shown very large because they were the windows of the soul. Your eyes tell me you only pretend to be tame. That you are still very wild.'

My turn to lie on my back and look up at the sky and the leaves overhead.

'You are like a tired sea, aren't you? Slapping for ever on the cliffs. Getting tired, wild, gentle, in turn. And also wise. I like wise people. I feel safe with them.'

'Nice compliment. Tired sea thanks you most awfully.'

'Sleep if you want to. You watched over me, why not me over you? Go on, sleep.'

'Tired sea no sleep.'

'Never?' she whispered.

'Never.'

She fell over my chest and we looked into each other's eyes, windows of the soul, weighing each other up.

'And you are like fire, aren't you?'

'Am I?'

'That's what I think,' I told her softly.

'You could be right, you could be wrong,' she murmured.

'I think I'm right. Sometimes you burn out, leaving just a few coals buried in the ashes. Sometimes a wind comes and you blaze.'

'If you are water and I'm fire we are not much use to each other, are we?'

'Aren't we? We can quench each other.'

I saw in her eyes that there was a fire burning. She saw the storm in my soul. We could never hurt each other, just quench the need in us. As we undressed I thought the old hermit of a tree chuckled to itself. We made very slow love at the foot of the tree. If the nomads had come they would have speared us – with justification. We looked and felt awkward with slacks, knickers, trousers and underwear bunched up at the ankles. What a pair. Wildebeestes have more dignity, mounting in the plains. But we were a couple of lost creatures, no longer sure about right and wrong. Perhaps no longer really caring. And we were defying the plains. It was unexpected and unplanned. A fire being quenched, a sea being made still. 'Can you feel me?' she asked.

'Yes.'

'Happy?'

'Yes.'

A child at the breast. Biting, sucking; what ecstasy! Wait till some morons come and spear the writhing bottoms. Nobody has any right to do this here. This place here is for nomad cattle and wild beasts. Not for women in crimplene slacks and responsible gentlemen from the city.

Welded together. Till we are no longer young and cannot run across the plains. Till we are two old animals chewing cud in the shade. Welded together.

Her lungs heaved as the bellows within her worked up the fire, worked up the fire. A storm was raging within me, and she could take all of it.

'You are damn good,' she said.

'Am I?'

'The only thing you are good at,' she said, 'and it's good for your belly, you know. Good for the abdomen muscles. At least better than nothing. Oh, it's beautiful, so good. Don't stop, never stop.'

She closed her eyes and a pained expression came on her face. Tears burst up between her eyelids and she began to weep. Ecstasy or sorrow?

'Don't stop, it's all right. You are all that is left, Matthew. Everything else is gone. I wish I could die, sometimes.'

'That's wrong to wish.'

'I know, Matthew. Hold me tighter. Make me all yours.'

'That's what I want you to be. All mine. For ever.'

'That's good. So good.'

Overcome, her fragile breast heaved up, fighting back the sea. Then a cry in the plains as she yielded. She shivered in my arms as I watched. The flame within her died slowly and reluctantly and she fell back, exhausted.

I waited for a while. She looked at me between half-closed eyelids and smiled. 'I didn't feel you come,' she panted.

'No, I didn't.'

'Why not? Go on, have it.'

'Are you on pills?' I asked. Always practical.

'Yes. There's nothing to fear. Go on. Come, Matthew. Come to me.'

Chapter Eight

A couple caring for each other deeply. We walked back to the car in the evening wind and I was paying for having left my jacket in the car.

'What if we find the car gone?' she asked. 'Will you run stark raving mad?'

'I know it's there. It's got to be there, I'm blistered.'

'And you must be feeling cold, too,' she said, her arm round my waist.

'Sort of.'

'I think I can see the car. It's still there.'

Suppose it had disappeared, I thought idly. We would be exposed to the chilling cold of the plains. We would have to walk at least five miles in twilight and darkness. Sinking low from the heights of bliss to the threshold of pain. It could easily happen, it was always happening to people. Every minute, every second, a creature was suffering, a creature was dying. And here we were feeling that the whole universe was in harmony. This was only a moment, and it was transient. All the more to be valued.

It was good to sit in the car. To lean towards each other and share a kiss. But I felt insecure. I fastened my seat belt and asked her to do the same.

'I never bother with it,' she said, with a little laugh.

She never bothered with it . . . Didn't give a damn if she was thrown out of the windscreen. Which was always happening. Pretty girls were always being thrown out of windscreens.

I fastened the belt for her. I reversed the car and drove away, the dust following. June remembered she had sweets in her handbag and peeled one for me.

'Good for a dry mouth,' she said. We drove on, sucking sweets Good for a dry mouth. Yes.

'What are you thinking about?' she asked.

'Our next move.'

'What do you want to do?'

'I don't know,' I said.

'Now I need to eat,' she said. 'Something appetising.'

'Where can we eat? There's nothing in my place.'

'We can go down to town. Have dinner and a drink.'

'And then what?' I asked.

'Take me to my flat.'

'And then what?'

'I sleep,' she said.

'And then?'

'Don't be silly.'

We drove on, dust furiously following.

'Bumpy road, isn't it?' she said.

'Yes. Am I too fast?'

'No. But I would like to know what is on your mind.'

I said, 'I want you to promise that you are not going back to the States. That you are going to stay here in Kenya and marry me.'

June sat still in her seat, staring at the road ahead.

'We can't talk about it now.' she said at last. 'Not in a moving car, and on a bumpy road.'

This seemed like our special day, and we decided to make the most of it. We dined in one of these places where waiters actually bow to you as they hand you the menu, and where along with the grub you are expected to pay service charge and tip the waiter.

'It's almost a crime to waste money like this,' June remarked as we studied the incredible menu, 'but I guess I owe you a meal. Choose anything.'

'I thought I brought you here. It's all on me.'

'I don't think you knew what you were in for. This is a trap for tourists. They milk them in here when they are still not used to thinking in terms of the local currency. And it's dead cheap for them, anyway. Since I feel like a tourist myself I insist on paying.'

As I wasn't all that loaded I didn't argue too much. We ate and had a drink and the bill came to forty bob and something over. All for a special day, of course. For those chandeliers, for the marble floor and the smart carpet, for the obsequiousness of waiters in tail coats, for the deathly hushness, for the privilege of being among so many well manicured people.

'For that amount I know places we can buy a whole lamb,' I moaned.

'Come on, don't be sour. I'm nowhere near being broke. As I'm not buying any land now I don't even know what I'll do with all the money.'

'Where did you get it anyway? I can't say I had anything like a fortune when I came back from United States. The almighty dollar was terribly evasive to me all the time I was there.'

She smiled airily as she said, 'I did a lot of modelling for magazines and commercials. I'd have hit it quite big, if I had wanted.'

'Oh? I'm quite awed. Modelling.'

'I earned quite a tidy sum. If my father had waited . . . but I won't cry any more for spilt milk. I'll try to get rid of the bitterness. But I'm terribly unforgiving. You know that? I'm plotting on how to get my own bit of satisfaction. Like going away for more study and never coming back. Or coming back loaded with money and doing things to make my materialistic father turn ashen with envy.'

My heart sank. Me and my father had her land and had refused to sell. We were guilty. We were sending her back. She must not go back, she must marry me. What a mess. My old man would never yield; and this girl was headstrong and out for some strange revenge. Where did that leave Matthew? Somewhere in the middle as usual. Wherever there was a battle of wills going on you could safely bet Matthew would be somewhere in the middle, confused and feeling all the pain. Here he was having his soul wrung and twisted.

I began to feel very depressed. So she was going back to the

USA to model. . . . Bloody USA. Always stealing the best. I suppose you screw her inbetween telling her which way to swing the leg. The agent made love to her, no doubt. Peel off that knicker and let's see what kind of leg you've got. That's swell, baby, just swell. Now if you'll just give me a screw and sign here. . . . A curse upon you. A dark African curse. For stealing the love of my childhood.

June lit a cigarette. Maybe she was that type who smoked only after a meal. She smiled. 'Still brooding over that bill?'

'Damn that bill,' I said viciously.

'Something is bothering you,' said my pretty tormentor.

'Maybe I need another beer.'

'Go ahead. Have it, Matthew.'

I stared at the empty bottle in front of me. There was no consistency in life, was there? This was a bottle of beer. There were places it cost half the price. This was a girl in front of me, not very much prettier than some I had conquered, not as pretty as some I had dropped, but with some frightening power over me.

'We won't have the second drink here,' I said suddenly.

'I was just beginning to get used to the atmosphere. It's deliciously civilised.'

I must smile. I must shake off this evil mood. I must appreciate what I have now. I must remember she came only the other day to mind her own business. For the first time she looks cheerful, and it's all up to me. I must not start ruining it all. If she walked away I would be the loser. And she could – easily. She's that type of girl. *A kind of car that ejects the driver and leaves him bleeding on the road.* Albert S. Kago was right, as usual.

'I know one or two good night-clubs,' I said. 'We could go and dance.'

She laughed. 'You're awfully fond of dancing aren't you? I'm not so sure I share your enthusiasm. But if you think it will cheer you up we could go. But I think you are tired, Matthew. All that driving, walking and other things I won't mention in decent society. I think you are ready for bed.'

'We won't stay long.'

'All right.'

We rose and I followed her out. A waiter smiled and I tried to smile back. The world was unjust, but you must still show them a tooth.

We went to the car. The night was cold, full of evil flashing lights.

'Matthew,' she said softly, 'do you mind . . . I really don't feel like dancing. Have a heart. I'm tired, if you are not. On top of that I'm not clean, I'm sweaty and feeling sick at the idea of jumping around.'

'What do you want?'

'Take me home. Please.'

There was only one way to bridge the gap between our souls, one way to ease the pain. I grabbed her and pulled her suddenly to me. Our lips met and I kissed her violently. Every frustrated male at one time or the other has to try and assert his power over the female. Cocks know the trick. Who the hell was this June? Just another bitch. A little headstrong but still a bitch. And I dug my claws into her breasts to assure myself I was right. I squeezed them until she felt the power in my hands, my masculine hands, which could be cruel if frustrated too much. I grabbed the flesh around her hips as we kissed, and ran my probing fingers up the thighs she had parted for me earlier on. In a fierce kiss I vented some of my anger and aggression.

She played up to me as well as she could, knowing I needed it, knowing I couldn't be stopped. She used her fingernails to crawl at my neck as her own fire surged within her. Traffic lights flashed over our faces but we went on and on, my anger melting into desire. Until somewhere we met on one level and stopped, looking at each other. Smiling as we assessed and studied each other. Some kind of shyness had gripped us, as if we had broken new ground, that demanded a change in the mode of communication. Words failed us both and we stared at our dimly-lit hands having their own embarrassed communion.

She was very sensitive and polite. She knew I'd be upset if she tried to hurry me. She gave me all the time I needed to search my own soul. She was very well developed as a woman, I thought. Knew exactly when to provoke, when to submit, when to make peace. The challenge was upon me. How good was I as a man? Could I prove I was her kind of man? Could I win her over and keep her? It was up to me to prove myself. At that moment I felt extremely unworthy. Very vulnerable. She was not going to be won through sulking and loss of temper. I wasn't sure what was needed. Maybe it was great gentleness, maybe it was cold reasoning and logic. I wasn't sure. And I was afraid of failure. Very much afraid.

'Tell me,' I said as we sat there in the car, 'that moment in the plains . . .'

'Yes?'

'Did you mean everything you said?'

'What did I say? Remind me.'

'You wept and said I was the only thing left. You seemed very much afraid of life and even wished you could die. Was it just a passing mood?'

'I suppose so. I get these moods. In the height of happiness I feel suddenly depressed.'

'And life loses meaning?'

'Yes. But the moods don't last anyway,' June said.

I thought for a while. 'When you said I was the only thing left . . .'

'That's true, you know. To me life is like a waiting-room. You sit and wait with strangers. Everybody is a stranger – even your own family. People come into the room and then disappear. Some keep reappearing. Like you, for instance. You reappear and begin to become sort of familiar.'

'Sort of familiar . . .'

'Even when you leave the room I can still see your face clearly, and even sense an emptiness in the room.'

'But in the end you are waiting alone?'

'That's right.'

'For what?'

'For something scaring, something frightening.'

I started the engine. I reversed from the kerb into the road. 'Do you mind if we have a drink before I take you to your flat?'

'No,' she said quickly, 'of course not.'

She was eager to please. Eager to compensate for another demand she could not fulfil. I had referred to her as my fiancée-to-be. Now I wasn't that confident. To make things worse, what had been said in half-jest was turning into a dead serious affair. I didn't want her now just to give anybody a grandson. She had, in a short space of time, become an essential part of me. To lose her would be to undergo a painful amputation in the soul. That was how I felt now in the dimly illuminated streets of Nairobi.

I drove down University Way. 'Do you know the Superview Lodge?' I asked. She shook her head. 'That's where I stayed just after coming back from America. They have a nice quiet bar and we can drink there.' I tried to make my voice bright and cheerful. She didn't comment.

Things got brighter when we got to the Lodge. I met two chaps I knew from the days I was staying there. A couple of lively bachelors who seemed to earn their money just for the pleasure of lazing around in the bar drinking beer, playing the juke-box and competing against each other in games of darts. The four of us sat at one table and serious issues were soon forgotten. Their sense of humour soon had June and me in hysterics. They told us how there had been a power failure the previous Friday. Runo, the short wiry one, told us how he had, before the bartender's eyes had been accustomed to the blackout, joined him behind the counter quietly and extracted several bottles of spirits from the cabinet, passing them on to his friend Chege. They crept to their room and counted their spoils. Two brandies, one Cinzano, two vodkas, all large bottles. They had no regrets: after all those years they had lived in the Lodge they felt the management owed them something.

'We have been drinking ourselves stupid the whole week but haven't gone half-way through the stuff. It's boring drinking in the room, you know. But now that you people are here, how about us going to my room to have some free booze instead of wasting money here?' The offer was from Runo. June, smiling, declined politely but emphatically. The two boys looked at each other and shrugged. When the offer came up again half an hour later we were too drunk and indebted to resist and we found ourselves in Runo's small room drinking the stolen spirits and listening to their endless jokes. Somewhere in the drunken course of the evening the boys found out that June's twenty-first birthday was in a week's time. They came out with what seemed to me to be a brilliant suggestion – a grand party for June. June protested, saying she never celebrated birthdays, but the three of us insisted and went ahead with the plans. I took great pains to draw a detailed map showing where my house was so that Runo and Chege would know how to get there with their small car loaded full of girls and liquor. 'Not stolen this time, we promise.' To show how serious they were (they had developed a warm affection for June) each boy fished out a pound as a pledge that they were in it to the hilt and slapped it on my willing hand. June sat on the bed, her body, leaning back on the wall, too overwhelmed by numbers and too tipsy to really protest.

It was about midnight when we finally left them. They came with us to the car and waved us off.

'You horrible people,' she murmured to me. But I could see she was happy. It had been a long but exciting day for her. 'A party on Saturday for me! I hope when you all wake up sober you'll realise it's ridiculous.'

'Why? When I was twenty-one I had a big party.'

'Where were you then?'

'Canada.'

'One of those student parties.'

'It was quite a big party, actually.'

'How many years ago was this?'

'Seven. I'm quite an old man.'

'Yes, you ought to be marrying somebody.'

'Does it mean I haven't proposed to you up to now? I must have given you the hint that I want you to stay and marry me.'

She laughed. 'How come you always bring up this subject when we are in a moving car . . . and on a bumpy road? Must be something peculiar in you, Matthew.'

I laughed. 'All right, I'll wait till we are somewhere where I can go on my knees and kiss the corns on your toes. How did you like the two boys?'

'A very immature pair, but quite irresistible. I'll never forget I drank some stolen liquor.'

'They feel the management has been indirectly stealing from them for the five years they have been there. To rob people a business man only needs to raise prices or fix new rents.'

'Yes, but the idea of Runo slipping behind the counter and helping himself to the drinks makes me think he's got the natural instincts of a born thief. Watch him when he comes to your house.'

'Oh, the boy is all right.'

'Which way are you going, Matthew? This is not Ngong Road.'

'Relax, June.'

'Where are you taking me?'

'Not a very strange place. Only to my house.'

Chapter Nine

When I look back I sometimes find it difficult to believe that it all happened. That she came and stayed in my house. The whole thing has the unreality of a dream; in fact I find it difficult to remember what exactly we did and in what order. Mine is the same plight as that of a holidaymaker who goes to a strange enchanting place where everything is crisp and fresh and new: then he comes back to the prosaic old surroundings and the images in his memory begin to cloud over with a perplexing rapidity. Anxious to preserve the memories and the fading emotions he digs with frantic fingers into a mass of old photographs. After a while even the photographs fail to revive the failing light of memory. They lose their stimulative value and become simply crinkled statements to the effect that indeed such and such a moment existed but it's gone, as all moments must. For you can't hold a moment.

Perhaps it's just as well that there are no photographs, for my mind longs not to remember but to forget. That's why I have been drinking so hard in the last year . . . in all sorts of places . . . with all sorts of people. And the drinking doesn't help my belly one bit. She should see me now!

That some things seem a little funny is a good sign. It's encouraging that I can laugh and even tell a few friends of some of the things we did in those seven days. Like I bought a carpet, a small red carpet from the *Oriental Boutique*, so that we didn't have to keep on using a blanket for our Yoga exercises. I don't quite know the effect the word 'Yoga' has on friends of mine like Albert Kago. When I tell them we used to do Yoga in my large sitting-room they look at me from the corner of their eyes as if I had narrowly missed insanity. Yet those Yoga exercises are the one precious thing I can moan about without the fear of being branded sentimental. I did feel a change in my belly in those seven days we did intense Yoga and intense love-making on that carpet. And I can say my affection for June is justified before the eyes of the coldest man by this one fact: that if that Yoga instructor of mine had stayed in my house for one whole year I would have achieved the fantastic isolation of the recti! But she left me far too early, even before I had enough of a base from which to plough on towards that shining goal. A comment on my will-power: one calm day I took a walk in town and bought a book entitled *Yoga Made Easy* and took it affectionately into the office. To my delight while leafing through it I saw an exercise I could do, as the book said, while at my work in the office or while waiting for traffic lights to show green. It was a simple exercise of hollowing the belly to help break down adipose tissue. I took the book to my house, my abdominal tissues already aching pleasantly with the efforts of the quiet afternoon. I spread the forgotten carpet on the floor so I could try a few exercises, but it was no use. A couple of stains on the carpet reminded me of June's brown naked flesh writhing under my own, of her voice whispering, teasing, or firmly instructing. No, the wound was not healed. I broke down and staggered into the kitchen to pour myself a brandy. So much for Yoga. And maybe now it's too late. I'm going on to thirty and the circumference of my girth seems to be obeying the dictates of a gland gone haywire. Isolating the recti seems like one of the many futile dreams that have gone in and out of my mind, driving me on faster to my fate as a drunken cynic.

'Don't you worry,' says Albert S. Kago. 'You bought shares in the Kenya Breweries, didn't you? You and I have fat shares in the breweries, and we don't want them broke, do we? Have another beer on me and don't be silly, mate!'

So I drink. I need the beer and I need Kago's company. But as I stare at the murals on the wall or at the bar calendar I seem to hear her voice saying, 'Beer is terribly fattening, you know, Matthew. From now on I want you to ration.'

There was nothing she told me to do that I couldn't do. She could have made me a superman. Was it some hidden magic in her or was I weak? Let's hear a cool, unbiased attempt at an analysis.

It's June's twenty-first birthday. Things are really warm. It's only about three o'clock in the afternoon but there are already about fifteen people in the room. I'm tipsy and very very content. Percy Sledge is singing *Warm and Tender Love* on my stereo. I'm dancing with my secretary Mumtaz, who astonished and delighted me by agreeing to drive here with me after work, provided she could leave at no later than six o'clock. Other couples dancing: June with a tall bearded fellow who came with somebody or other and whose name I forget; Runo with a small cuddlesome Danish volunteer he ran into the other night and whom he has already taken to bed; Chege is dancing with his own bottle in a corner because the only girl who isn't dancing is holding hands with a fellow in the verandah. This is the first party ever held in the house and it's going extremely well. A couple of handsome birthday cards lie on the TV set. One small funny one from Chege and Runo completely overshadowed by Mumtaz's huge red one that shows an elegant wreath of flowers and a silver key. Mumtaz, who is not yet twenty-one herself, has written with a hint of jealousy, 'Now you are twenty-one and the key to the door of self-knowledge is yours now by right. All the best.'

As I dance with Mumtaz I smile in amusement and I tease her about the message. 'You think she's like you? Frightened and obedient? June snatched the key when she was about nineteen.'

'I know,' said Mumtaz. 'But don't forget your culture is in a melting-pot.'

'What melting-pot?'

'I mean, there aren't any rigid rules these days. Everybody understands there is a wind of change, and they don't insist that you act like this or like that. No Asian girl, for example, can act the way she does.'

'How does she act?' I follow up, lightly, for there's nothing I enjoy more than seeing Mumtaz's eyes bright and large as she tries to convince someone about something she strongly believes.

'She's so free, you know. She can go anywhere, do anything. Even live with you, like she's doing.'

'Yes, she and I believe in doing what we feel is right. We don't turn to anybody for guidance on matters that concern our two souls.'

'Yes, but the credit is not due entirely to you and your intelligence. Your society as a whole has learnt to reserve judgement, after the old values have been proved inadequate. So she's helped that way. If I tried to be like her I'd have a mental breakdown because of the pressures I would face.'

'Would you like to be as free as her and do the things she's doing?'

She smiled mischievously. 'Like sleeping with you, for instance? No.'

'You don't find me attractive?'

'Let's change the topic. I don't want her to claw my eyes out.'

'She doesn't fight.'

'No. I think I know her character.'

'Don't be too sure. She's complicated.'

'I know that. I know she's complicated.'

I stared in amusement into her large eyes. If I was an Asian and a Moslem I would go all out to get Mumtaz. She's a joy.

'You seem pretty certain you know her. You were sitting next to her I remember. And I suppose you made sure you stole a long look at her palm.'

She laughed. 'Actually I did that,' she confessed.

'And what did you discover?'

'That's she's very wilful. Not as sentimental as you.'

'You keep telling me that I'm sentimental. But I think I'm hard. Very hard.'

'You can't be. You're a Pisces. It's perhaps the softest sign in the Zodiac. If her birthday is today she's Leo. Pisces and Leo don't match. You can harmonise with just about anybody who is pleasant. And you can tolerate unpleasant types. She chooses her friends with care and is awfully ambitious.'

'She's ambitious. Wants to get a PhD. Wants to become a model. She would want to become a film star too, if Hollywood gave her a chance.'

74

'She's very fiery, you know,' said Mumtaz, swaying with the gentle music and concentrating deeply. I had poured a little quantity of Vodka into her glass of Fanta and she had complained that it was too strong. I wondered what effect it was having on her. Not to worry. The stuff hardly smelled.

She went on, 'If you married, you'd find her the stronger partner. You would have to let her have her way quite often.'

'You're telling me. Look at that TV set. It was at the opposite end of the room. I came home from work and I found the whole room changed. We had a small argument on aesthetics and I let her win it.'

'You must give in when you can, Matthew,' Mumtaz advised, 'or you'll frustrate her so much she'll want to quit. They are always looking for the ideal, people of her star.'

'Well, she's got her ideal, hasn't she?'

'Has she?' Mumtaz asked sceptically. 'The ideal is unattainable, isn't it? A whole series of mirages.'

'You think I'm one of the mirages she's going to see on the horizon as she trudges on through the desert of existence.'

'You have put it very poetically and very correctly.'

'Have I any hope of keeping her?'

She shook her head. 'Very slim. From the facts you have told me about her.'

'She might stay, Mumtaz.'

'She might?'

'Yes. At first she was thinking only of going back to the States. But in the week we have stayed together here she has begun to trust me – even depend on me. She is very happy.'

'Yes, I think she loves you quite a little bit. And you?'

'She's my whole life.'

'I hope she stays, Matthew,' said Mumtaz gently.

'Yes. I hope she stays.' I smiled as I looked at June dancing with the tall bearded fellow. 'Things are not going too badly, are they? We have just completed a week together. First Great Week!'

If anybody had told me that it would also be our last week I would have argued hotly. If anybody had told me that this was our last day, that tomorrow night she wouldn't sleep here, I would have told him to simply piss off and stop bugging me. Yet this party was destined to end on a very tragic note.

I remember that evening more clearly than anything else. The party went on beautifully, everybody dancing freely, everyone very friendly. There was a certain magic in the air, a very deceptive, devilish magic, perhaps. The crowd was my type of crowd – good mixers, good drinkers, all of them at heart gentle and unpretentious. The room had recently been painted, and June, bending to the inevitable, had accompanied me that morning to town and bought paper decorations which were now hanging in the room, enhancing the atmosphere. A few balloons also, one of which the mischievous Runo had blown up with a glowing cigarette just to startle a few girls. June had made my heart glow warmly by asking me to take her out for a breath of air and we had gone among the coffee trees hand in hand, and stood for a good ten minutes kissing as if we had just met. 'I love you very much,' I had told her and she had said, 'I know, Matthew. And that is good. I'm happy.' And everything else seemed to be happy. The breeze blowing through the coffee, the old house with its new paint and its very first party, the cypress trees, the coffee. It was as if the whole farm was alive and happy. Sounds like the words of a pop song, but I don't know how better to put it. I felt convinced she would never leave me, that this atmosphere would last for eternity – at least until one of us died, and even then something would remain, for the grave would be among the cypress trees. The half of us that would linger on could walk among the trees and somehow communicate with the spirit of the dead one. But I could not conceive at that sacred moment the possibility of our ever parting. Maybe I'm the type which, whenever anything glints, wants to believe it's gold. I want to believe it's gold until the cold experts prove it's not.

After we went back inside we danced only with each other, as if after tuning up the world to our own happy note we had to be together for our own duet. And then Mumtaz touched my shoulder. 'Six o'clock, Matthew,' she said.

A quick signal passed between the three of us.

'Let's drive Mumtaz to town, June.'

'Sure,' she said.

Poor Mumtaz. Standing there in a sari, staunch, brave, apologetic. A lonely lagoon bleeding through the sandbank into the sea of life. Poor Mumtaz. With her broken life-line. Hope palmistry is all wrong Hope it's all bullshit.

I left the two of them talking for a moment and went to tell Runo. I told him not to let the atmosphere sag, June and I were coming back.

'We are running out of booze,' he said. 'Bring some more.'

He slipped me a couple of pounds, which I reluctantly took, for I had enough money of my own. I then went into the kitchen for a case of empties, and gripping it in my hands nodded to the two girls to follow. We drove Mumtaz to Nairobi West and deposited her at a safe distance and left her to go on alone to her uncle's place. Then I exchanged the empty case for a full one and we drove back.

And then a whole dream came to an end – or received the first crushing blow. Coming back to the house we met my old man walking slowly up the drive towards the road. A sickening feeling came upon me. I had forgotten all about him. Like a habitual criminal forgets the cops until they trap him in an ambush. I wondered whether to stop or just wave to him and go on. June had also frozen in her seat, sensing trouble. She sat back in her seat with an ironical smile, fearing the worst. I stopped the car.

He looked very grey and old as he stared for a moment at the ground at his feet. He was on June's side of the car and he looked past her at me. His eyes chilled me, made by guts recoil. Imagine a meeting between Gabriel and one of hell's angels. An unplanned meeting in which nothing has been rehearsed and no one has been briefed.

'Why did you stop?' he asked. 'Did you want to talk to me?'

What is there to answer when your own father asks you that? I just kept quiet and stared back at him.

'Well, come out and have a talk with me,' he suggested. 'You stopped, so I must assume you want to talk.'

He was looking past June as if she wasn't there. Yet he must know her as Joshua's daughter. Maybe that was the trouble. The sin was too great for him to acknowledge.

I got out of the car and we both walked to the back of it.

'You are drunk, aren't you? Say yes or no, so I know what to tell you without wasting any words.'

First time I had seen him hostile since I had been accepted as a grown-up. First time in my life I had seen him really angry.

'I'm not very drunk,' I said. 'Speak and I will understand.'

His look was very violent as he measured me up from head to foot. I also measured him up myself – much more politely because he was sixty-five and because I was just a small seed from his loins. He had all the advantages. He had God with him. And I had the bat.

'You dare do this to me!' he hissed.

'Do what?' I inquired politely.

'Turn my house into a den of thieves.'

'I'm just having a party.'

My cool tone made his anger overshoot its mark and vanish from his head for a moment to be replaced by numbing shock. Some fathers can't bear to be talked back to. They want you to bow your head contritely and prepare for some abuse. Like an animal being mounted. Show them you've got a penis and they don't like it.

He began to shake like he had been struck by a severe bout of malaria. Somehow, with the help of beer I could detach a part of my mind (the sober part) and allow it to hover around the scene and observe. It kept reporting that nobody was to blame, nobody was at fault. The meeting shouldn't have happened, that was all. We were two very different animals, that was all. He was quite right to shake like this, so let him shake. I was quite right to stand there without a prick of conscience.

'Do you know what I have just seen?' he demanded, like one who had seen a ghost. 'Somebody vomiting on the grass. You've turned my house into Sodom and Gomorrah.'

I wondered who had vomited. One or two chaps, drinking the free booze rather greedily, had looked pretty sick to me. But vomiting, among those of us who indulge in the stuff, is quite normal, so I found it hard to tremble with him.

'Did you come back here to shame me? Did you come here to bring evil upon my house?'

'No.'

'Why did you come, Matthew?'

'You invited me. You wanted me to come and live here.'

Perhaps now you sympathise with my father. I grew up a rather difficult child, always giving the wrong type of answer.

'Did I invite you along with your beer? And your women?'

'No.'

Triumphantly he cocked his thumb towards June. 'Who is that woman?'

'A friend.'

'Did I invite her here also?'

'No.' I said. I realised that he did not know it was Joshua's daughter in the car. If he had seen her around the place she had been, like now, in a jacket and slacks, and a very different June from the quiet little girl he had known. And he was getting old, anyway.

He stopped trembling and pulled himself together.

'Matthew, the neighbourhood is talking. Everyone is talking. I have been keeping quiet myself but after what I have seen today I can keep quiet no longer. What sort of people are in there?'

'Friends of mine.'

'Are your friends like that? Drunkards?'

'This is a party.'

'A party, eh? Let me tell you something. This farm is thirteen acres in size. There is a fence round it. You can see the fence. Inside that fence I have invited the Lord and embraced him with my hands Do you hear me? The Lord rules over my farm. The Lord protects my farm. The Lord gave my farm to me. All of the thirteen acres.'

He was sweating now and speaking in utter conviction. 'If you do not care for the Lord it's up to you,' he said, 'but you must not bring the devil to me. Keep him outside my fence. That's all I can say, Matthew. Act accordingly.'

Suddenly he was very calm, He was now a father with a son who had erred standing in front of him. And the son wasn't a small boy but a man of twenty-eight.

'I don't want the people to talk about you and your ways any more. And I don't want people to talk about me. I want you to think about that. You know where you have gone wrong. I want you to correct it. I want my house clean. I want the Lord back into my house. And I want him back soon.'

Let's skip over the next three or four uncomfortable hours that followed, with June and me sharing a sombre secret that the others did not know. We wanted them out quickly so we could talk and decide on a line of action, but the evening was out of our control now. The fresh cargo of liquor added fuel to the flames and June and I sat holding hands in a corner, our grief and our dismay unnoticed. There was a deep silent communication between us. We were two outsiders wholly dependent on one another for comfort, and she almost snarled at the bearded fellow when he came stone drunk to her, wanting her to leave my side and dance with him. I, my father's decadent son, sat on our Yoga carpet, drinking myself silly, and experiencing a strange mixture of sorrow and bliss. I was wholly understood by her who shared the carpet with me, and totally misunderstood by the world outside. I have a taste for melodrama, and I felt like a rebel with a cause. And I had my woman and my gang. As the night went on I played my role with a certain air of recklessness, tossing empty bottles aside and asking my faithful woman for more. I fell asleep, leaning against the wall, and when I woke up there was only June bending over me and telling me that the last couple had gone and that I should rise up and go with her to bed.

The earth tilted over and it was morning. I was woken up by a curious sound as if a radio had been turned on before transmission time. In the space between space and wakefulness the sound worried my subconscious mind, for it kept on coming and going like the mewling of a cat, like the cry of a soul in pain.

When I finally woke up June was lying back against the fat

pillows running her slim finger round and round the rim of a stem-glass.

She smiled at me. 'Did I wake you up?'

'What the hell are you doing?'

'Thinking. And amusing myself.' Again she ran her finger round the rim of the glass and the whining sound came back into the room. It was like she was gathering the silence of the room and concentrating it together till it sought release in transmutation into high frequency sound.

'Very clever.' I remarked.

She stopped her little game and sipped at the whisky in the glass. 'Want some?' she asked and brought the glass to my lips. 'It will do some good to your hangover.'

'I must have been very drunk last night,' I remarked.

'Very. Drink it all. I've got half a bottle on the floor.'

I gulped the whisky and sighed. I gave the glass back to her and she refilled it with neat whisky.

'I'm glad you woke up at last,' she said. 'We have to be going pretty fast.'

I lay there looking at the ceiling. Yes, she had to go. It was inevitable. I remembered the encounter with my father. The neighbourhood was talking about me and her, so she had to go. At the back of my mind I suppose I had expected a crisis but I had not realised it could come so suddenly and brutally. And it wouldn't have ended like this but for the party. I had taken a great risk without anticipating the full consequences that could arise.

We lay there gulping whisky. She kept on running a finger round the glass to produce her sound. She stared at the glass and I stared at her handsome profile. There was no question of parting from her, she was mine. I ran my hands over her breasts. I had a splitting, throbbing headache after last night's excesses but I was thinking hard. Her flat in Jamhuri Estate had been given to somebody else by Kago and all her things were here. I had encouraged her to give up the flat and even promised her I would get Kago to refund some of the advance money she had paid. I had been so confident that we could stay here together without being disturbed. So the neighbourhood had had their eyes fully open. Over the week they had seen us going down town together – June to libraries and me to work. Yes, that dumb looking crowd waiting at the bus stop, watching us pass by without giving them a lift. Mbathia's son and Joshua's daughter. A conceited pair from abroad, sticking together and trying to keep everybody (including God, the only one who can unite man and woman) totally out of their lives. Yes, it was easy to see how it had spread. We were a rather conspicuous couple, no matter how low we tried to hide. And the neighbourhood must have a lot of spite for us, for the way we lived, asking for licence from neither God nor man. Was that what happened to people when they got too highly educated?

Yes, we must have had a lot of guts to carry on like that! But now it had to stop. It just had to. We had to part or move somewhere else. Well, we couldn't part. I couldn't bear the thought.

'We'll have to find a hotel, now,' I said.

'We? You don't have to move. It's me who has to.'

'Oh, come on, June. You know you can't leave me here alone.'

'Why not?'

'Why not, you ask? I'm used to you. On top of that I love you.'

'So?'

'Wherever you are going I'm going.'

She smiled. 'Are you quoting a verse from the Old Testament? Who said that? "Wherever you are going I'm going . . ."'

'I'm dead serious. This house means nothing to me without you.'

'You were quite happy before I came,' she said, still running her hand round the rim and producing that relentless sound. 'You were quite happy, weren't you?'

'Don't talk like that, June. As if you don't know the facts. Night after night I've told you. About how things were before I met you. You know how happy I am with you. You know how miserable I would be if you went.'

'But I'm going, Matthew. I have to.'

'Not without me, June.'

'Oh, don't be ridiculous. I'm the homeless one. You are all right. You've got your house.'

'When it comes to that I'm also homeless,' I shot back. 'This is not my house. I didn't build it. If it was really my house nobody would move you from here that easily. Not even my beloved old father.'

'Want some more whisky?' She gave me the stem-glass. I lay with my left elbow supporting my weight and with the glass in my right hand. 'June, please. You just have to stop thinking in terms of us being two separate units. We have to plan together.'

'And this is what I have refused to do all along. I like you, Matthew. You are very good and very gentle. But you are wrong in certain things. We *are* two different individuals. You've got your life, I've got mine.'

Feeling bitter, I took a big gulp. I handed the glass back to her and lay back. I was very tired, very depressed. What was the point of talking? You can't change people's souls by mere talking. If she didn't love me enough she didn't.

Seeing how hurt I was she softened. She looked at me and said, 'Honestly, Matthew, I would like you to come with me but I'm not sure where I'm going. I suppose I'll have to book a hotel room in that noisy city. I can't go to Molo – I can't bear my father. I'm homeless, Matthew, and I mean it! Staying with you has been great, I must say that. It's a pity I have to go.'

I looked at her, trying to understand how she felt. Maybe she had a point. Maybe it was ridiculous for me to start packing up just to follow her. There was one good solution, but would she accept it?

'June, why don't we get married? I'm tired of asking.'

'Married. Just try to picture it, Matthew. As I was telling you the other night, I can't repeat my sister's nightmare. Can you imagine me being dressed up in that horrible dress? Surrounded by silly bridesmaids and being walked to some church? I'm an existentialist, not some Christian virgin, and the whole ceremony makes me sick. And the dowry bit is something I can't compromise with. My materialistic father would want to see me bought pretty dearly just because I have a BA. Forget marriage, I'm out of it, for now. Can't bear the hypocrisy of it all.'

83

'There are other ways to get married.'

'I know. I know, Matthew, but you also know that the pious neighbourhood wouldn't be satisfied with a marriage at the Registrar's office. My old father in Molo would go into a fit for passing him like that. There's no way to avoid unpleasantness. You just have to give people their wedding cake, you just have to let the preacher speak his lines, you just have to give the old man his bit of cash. I tell you, I'm out of it. And besides all that I'm just twenty-one, with plenty of opportunity to travel, study, make money, round up my life the way I want it. You boys can propose to me when I'm thirty, if you can still bear an old maid. I'm keeping my youth to myself.'

'You are terribly arrogant.'

'Yes.'

'Terribly selfish.'

'All of us are. I'm only selfish with my life. The moment I sign somewhere that I'm married to somebody it will never be my life. again. With all this African Socialism and extended family nonsense I'll be a creature without an independent soul. I'll be caught up in a net like my sister was. You know that white net thing brides wear when being escorted to church: I'd like to know its origin. It's so terrifying. There goes the pregnant bride, hemmed in on all sides. . . . No longer herself, but a creature bought with money. Let's not talk about it. It makes me shiver. And Matthew, let that be your last proposal, you are boring me.'

I was boring her. I, Matthew, a very gentle and loving fellow, was boring her.

'All right,' I said, feeling upset. 'I will never propose to you again.'

'You can, when I'm ready. If ever I'm ready. If ever I come back.'

'Kenya is your home, my dear. Even if you go, you must come back,' I said helplessly.

'Women are easily absorbed into other territories, Matthew. In the old days when you gentlemen used to wear skins and carry spears you used to capture girls from Ukambani and Masailand and bring them over to this side. And despite the fact that you had wiped up their village they stayed with you, learned your language, even learnt to love you. This primitive feeling of belonging to a certain territory all your life is stronger in men than in women. I could settle abroad easily, I hate to have to announce. But to be honest I don't think I will. One day I'll come back.'

'When is that, June?'

'When I'm old enough and mature enough to bear hurting people. At the moment I'm much too young and sensitive. I have to run away and hide in an impersonal society where I can do exactly as my soul tells me. Where nobody knows me enough to try and shape my life for me.'

I looked at her. 'Have you ever had a heart-break, June?'

'Yes, once when I was slightly younger and terribly immature. First boy I gave myself to broke my heart.'

'You are the first girl I've really given myself to – heart, body and soul. And I feel you've just broken my heart.'

Mischievously she put a hand on my heart.

'It's still beating.'

I had to smile. I looked at the face I loved. You can't have your cake and eat it, I thought. You can't get a girl and still love her, perhaps. Maybe I loved June because she had always been an inch or two beyond my reach.

We didn't talk any more. I took the glass from her hand and put it on the floor. I wrapped her in my arms and kissed her hungrily and desperately. She lay looking thoughtfully up at the ceiling as I kissed her neck, her breast, her navel. The gap between her soul and mine could never be bridged, perhaps, but I still had this privilege. Did she feel I deserved it, or was she simply being very kind to a slave? I took her with violence, interrupted with moments of almost tearful gentleness. She lay there, not terribly involved but full of infinite understanding and kindness. Passion rose in me in waves like those of the sea, angry tormented waves until at last I was spent and lay wearily upon her naked breast.

Chapter Ten

We slept in a modest hotel in town like two lonely fugitives. We drank and smoked in bed and lay listening to a juke-box playing not far away from our room. She was very much preoccupied and it was somewhat frustrating to lie there with her and not know what she was thinking about. Frustrating also to realise how very little she needed my help, even if she was alone in a predicament. I thought perhaps love-making would cheer her up or at least send her to sleep but for the first time she resisted my advances, saying she was not at all in the mood. I looked at my watch and saw that it was only eight o'clock in the evening.

'How about a drink?'

'No. Thanks, Matthew.'

'It's a bit too early to sleep, isn't it?'

'You can go to the bar and have a drink,' she said. 'Please do that. I feel a bit nervous with you here.'

'Nervous?'

She smiled. 'Don't be offended. It's just that I have so many things to think about and I can't worry about you and me at the same time. You look so bored and I'm sorry for you. You should have stayed up-country in your house, Matthew.'

'It's too quiet up there, you know. I used to hate it, and after this I'll hate it even more.'

'Yes, I'm worried about you. There is a certain air of helplessness around you. You need someone to mother you all the time.'

'Someone like you.'

'Perhaps. You know, I really wish I could stay. You are quite a fine man and I like you. I wish it wasn't all that complicated.'

'I wish so too,' I said simply. I would have proposed to her for the umpteenth time but I had been warned.

In the end I had to get up, dress and go to the bar. I ordered a beer and stood at the counter, among strangers, letting my mind just wander. I felt resigned now. I had lost the battle. She was like a slippery eel and she had finally slipped back into the waters. But there was still time to get accustomed to the idea of losing her. There were still a few weeks to spend together. So I thought.

The following morning I woke up, kissed her good-bye and left her in bed. I went to work, looking forward to meeting her for lunch at Tina's. Lunchtime came and I went to Tina's, but she didn't appear. I rang her hotel and someone told me she had checked out. But there was a note for me at the reception desk, if I would care to come and collect it. I hung up and drove to the hotel. The note said she had decided to go away for a while – not very far – just to relax a bit. She was feeling very depressed, although there was no reason why she should feel that way, and she thought a change of atmosphere would do her some good.

She went on: 'I also don't feel happy about your running away from home, where you belong. As I know you can't go back home when I'm around town I am off to the coast to give you a chance to forget me. I'm sorry to have caused you all the pain, Matthew, but when all is said and done I don't think either of us regrets our small episode. I'll be back in roughly two weeks and you can buy me that lunch at Tina's if you don't feel too mad at me.'

So I was alone again. The small episode, as she called it, was over and I was alone again. I ordered a meal and my usual lunchtime vodka and sat thinking about the whole affair. I wondered what I should do. I came to the conclusion that I should also go on holiday. Forget that house in the country for a while. Forget June, if I could.

That's really the end of the story, except that we met again for a few hours a couple of days after I had resumed work. I was in the office cursing the tropical heat of the afternoon when I heard Mumtaz talking with another girl. Then the door opened and the two came in together. They burst out laughing as they both stared at me.

'I bet her a bob that you'd faint at the sight of her, Matthew,' said Mumtaz, 'but you are a very cool one, aren't you?'

'Is this you or am I seeing things?' I asked June.

'I'll leave you two together,' Mumtaz said.

June closed the door after her. Smiling, she sat down. She was still the same old girl dressed casually in jeans.

'So this is you in all your glory, Matthew. This is a very smart office. What are all those papers?'

'Forget it. Let's talk about you. Where did you go to?'

'You first,' she said. 'Your secretary told me you went off somewhere. She also told me you looked very heart-broken but you look all right to me. You look very good, in fact.'

'Do I? Well, I went up north.'

'North where?'

'Isiolo district.'

She rolled her eyes. 'So far away. Must be about two hundred miles from here. How was it?'

'Very fine, actually. One former class mate is a District Officer there. I had a long-standing invitation. I drove up there myself. Quite tiring. I had to stop at Meru and spend the night at a hotel. Then I hit Isiolo early in the morning and met my friend.'

'Did he give you a good time?'

'Yes, he was going up to Merti on business and we went together.'

'Merti?'

'It's a place to the north-east of Isiolo; very remote place. The road is very rough and passes through dry scrubland full of wild life. You see lots of elephants and zebras and giraffes. It's a long, rough drive but it's very beautiful. So many beautiful ranges of blue mountains. You feel you are in the heart of Africa, and it's great. I wished you were there.'

She smiled. 'I think the trip did you good, Matthew. You look very healthy.'

'But I missed you, June. It's good to see you. Tell me where you went. I know you went to the coast, but where exactly?'

Her eyes sparkled. 'Nowhere, Matthew. I didn't go anywhere.'

'You mean . . .?'

'I simply changed my hotel. Moved a few yards down to another street.'

I jumped from my seat and paced around.

'You mean you were just hiding from me?'

'I thought it would do you good. And it did.'

'You cunning little bag of tricks. All the time I was up there in the north you were right here?'

'Yes, but I went to Molo for a few days to say good-bye to my folks.'

'When are you leaving?' I asked with a stab of pain.

'You won't believe it. But I'm leaving tonight.'

'Tonight?'

She nodded. 'Tonight, Matthew. Would you like the honour of escorting me to the airport?'

We spent the evening together and I drove her to the airport a couple of hours before the flight. While I was in Isiolo and Merti she had been busy preparing a rather complicated flight that would give her a chance to explore some major cities of Europe before proceeding to America. It might be three weeks before she actually got to Washington. In the airport lounge I watched her studying some maps and asked her, 'Aren't you scared?'

'Scared of what?'

'Of loneliness?'

'Not really. I've been lonely for so long, I become nervous when I'm not. By the way, are you back at your house?'

'Yes, I am. Back to the old life.'

'Marry somebody, Matthew,' she pleaded. 'Don't be a glum old bachelor for ever. Get a nice simple girl from the countryside who will look after your house and give your parents a grandson. Promise me.'

'All right. If one comes my way.'

She smiled. 'That's the spirit.' Then her face softened. 'I know I'm a fool. I know you could be good to me. Maybe one day I'll sit and regret that I didn't marry you. I'm sure I love you, but do we have to marry everybody we fall in love with? It's a very short life, Matthew, very short and I feel I must make the best of it. Please forgive me.'

'There is nothing to forgive. I think you are a great girl, June. I sometimes wish I had your courage. I wish I could leave my job and my house and roam like you. But like most people in the world I'm a coward, always seeking security, always clinging to life-preservers and never swimming into life itself. But come back, June. Some day.'

She placed her slim hand on mine to comfort me. 'I will, Matthew, I will.'

Not long afterwards her flight was announced and she vanished into the guts of the airport. I walked upstairs into the waving base and stood there in the cold night air waiting for the plane to leave.

It felt very odd to wave at the plane. June was probably unaware that I was there. As I watched the plane begin to taxi to the runway my limp hand fell to my side. The plane rushed down the runway and took off while friends and relatives of those inside waved and waved. Was she real or had she been a dream? It did not matter, she was gone. The pin-point lights of the plane disappeared into the night and the crowd began to walk away, murmuring. I walked away too. I went in search of something real. Like a beer, like a friend. I drove slowly through the quiet night towards the beckoning, gleaming lights of the town.